"YOU STAY AWAY FROM ME, YOU MENACE!"

George stopped, his expression a pitiful attempt at injured innocence. "What's wrong?"

The man had just kissed her into a terminal state of lust and he wanted to know what was wrong. Okay, she could do one of three things: She could jump his bones. She could strangle him. Or: "Go home."

He stared. "What?"

"You have to go home."

"Now?"

"If not sooner."

His voice dropped to that seductive purr Candy belatedly recognized as risky business. "Are you sure?"

No! cried her needy body. "Absolutely, positively," said her mouth.

Head tilted, he eyed her speculatively. Candy braced, half expecting him to pounce, half hoping he would, although she wasn't sure what she'd do to him if he did. Her circuits were still badly jumbled.

Then he walloped her with The Smile, and those circuits sizzled, popped, and blew.

"I'll go," he said. "For now."

He stalked off into the darkness, trailing testosterone, while Candy shivered in his wake. A single thought drifted through the wreckage of her peace of mind. *Uh-oh.*

WHAT ARE *LOVESWEPT* ROMANCES?

They are stories of true romance and touching emotion. We believe those two very important ingredients are constants in our highly sensual and very believable stories in the LOVE-SWEPT line. Our goal is to give you, the reader, stories of consistently high quality that may sometimes make you laugh, sometimes make you cry, but are always fresh and creative and contain many delightful surprises within their pages.

Most romance fans read an enormous number of books. Those they truly love, they keep. Others may be traded with friends and soon forgotten. We hope that each LOVESWEPT romance will be a treasure—a "keeper." We will always try to publish

LOVE STORIES YOU'LL NEVER FORGET
BY AUTHORS YOU'LL ALWAYS REMEMBER

The Editors

HUNTER
IN
DISGUISE

KATHY
DiSANTO

BANTAM BOOKS
NEW YORK · TORONTO · LONDON · SYDNEY · AUCKLAND

HUNTER IN DISGUISE

A Bantam Book / December 1997

ISBN 0-553-44628-2

Published simultaneously in the United States and Canada

---

*Bantam Books are published by Bantam Books, a division of Bantam Dou-
bleday Dell Publishing Group, Inc. Its trademark, consisting of the words
"Bantam Books" and the portrayal of a rooster, is Registered in U.S.
Patent and Trademark Office and in other countries. Marca Registrada.
Bantam Books, 1540 Broadway, New York, New York 10036.*

PRINTED IN THE UNITED STATES OF AMERICA

OPM   10 9 8 7 6 5 4 3 2 1

To Dad
In loving memory

ONE

It was a world-class tush. No, a Greek-god tush. It should be carved in marble and mounted in the Acropolis.

"Excuse me, may I speak to you for a minute, Mr. Price?"

Mile-wide shoulders stiffened. Like the tush, the shoulders were prime specimens of perfection. God had truly blessed this man with an incredible body.

"It'll have to wait, Ms. Johnson. I'm busy."

Of course the rest of him was classic jerk.

Exasperated by the attitude he seemed to reserve for her alone, Candy jammed one hand on her waist and canted a hip. Her head cocked as she pursed her lips. Any of the teenagers milling around on the volleyball court or scattered across the bleachers could have warned George Price that it was time to watch his step.

"I'm afraid it can't wait," she said. "I have to talk to you before class starts."

Heaving a sigh, he turned. At five-ten Candy

looked most men in the eye. Right now she really resented the fact that she had to look up to six-foot-three-inch Pinhead Price.

"All right, Ms. Johnson," he rumbled in that deep-as-the-ocean voice, "you have the floor."

Maybe, but it was a second before she could do anything with it, mostly because his voice never failed to ruffle her nerve endings and get her flustered. Evidently her ears didn't know the difference between a well-built moron and Sean Connery.

But after seven years' teaching experience, she had her poker face down pat. She would eat dirt and die before letting Price know he could give her goose bumps with one bass-clef word from those chiseled lips.

While her brain was numbed by his voice her eyes sneaked down to his chest, which was covered in a tight red Donnerton High T-shirt. Her eyes continued on up to skim his throat and granite jaw, snagging on the aforementioned chiseled lips before meeting his smart-aleck gray gaze.

At this point Candy barely suppressed a grimace.

God had coupled a mouthwatering face and body with a fashion flare that would have to stretch to be nonexistent. Price's clunky glasses were a sad blast from the long past. The nerd strap belting them to his thick skull bisected a black mane that might be impressive if it wasn't slapped flat with a pound of greasy kid's stuff.

His mouth curled into a snide grin. "Thinking of doing my portrait?"

Chagrined to be caught staring, Candy muttered, "I'd rather draw flies."

A disconcerting glint of something like amusement crept into his eyes. It was disconcerting because the ability to be amused indicated an intelligent life-form, and she wasn't sure Price qualified.

"Hmm. In that case, what can I do for you, Ms. Johnson?"

She really hated it when he called her Ms. Johnson in that snide tone. Disagreeable twerp.

"I'd like to talk to you."

"So talk."

"Not here. Would you mind stepping into the hall?"

He gave her a long-suffering look, and she battled a sudden urge to smack him with her clipboard. Her fingers tightened ominously, but she managed to check the impulse.

"Look, Ms. Johnson, this game between the boys' and girls' sixth-period classes was your idea. Personally, I don't think it's a good one. Anybody with half a brain in her head would know a bunch of women don't stand a chance against a few good men when it comes to sports."

"That's the most—"

He held up a finger. "But now that I've gone against my better judgment and agreed, I think we should get this cockeyed battle of the sexes under way." He smirked. "So I can prove my point."

The clipboard compulsion swelled to almost overwhelming proportions as she jerked her chin toward the door. "If you don't mind."

Pinhead shrugged and followed her across the hardwood floor, through the double doors, and into the hallway. Bracing one foot against the wall, he leaned back nonchalantly. The ball in his hands began a lazy rotation.

"Well, here we are in the hallway." He lifted an annoying eyebrow. "*Why* are we here in the hallway, Ms. Johnson?"

"We are here, George, to discuss your balls."

His eyes widened slightly. "Ah. I'm flattered, Ms. Johnson. I didn't think you'd noticed."

He certainly seemed intrigued now, the overgrown dip.

"It would be hard not to notice, what with them being the wrong ones and all."

The ball in his hands stopped spinning as intrigue segued into confusion. "The wrong ones?"

"You brought out the soccer balls. We're supposed to be playing volleyball." She smiled sweetly. "Remember?"

His foot plunked down on the floor. He looked at the ball. "Soccer balls?"

"Yes. You *do* know the difference, don't you? It adds up to about two pounds of air per square inch and half a dozen broken fingers."

He stuck out his chin, a tempting target, but she restrained herself. "I knew that."

I don't believe you, she thought suddenly. And that made her wonder.

Candy was good at wondering, suspecting, and hypothesizing. Because she'd never before had a genuine mystery to solve, her deductive-reasoning skills had yet to be tested, but she imagined she would be good at that too. Her investigative skills had been honed under the best: Conan Doyle, Christie, Spillane.

Some would call her a mystery-suspense junkie. Candy preferred to think of herself as a brilliant sleuth trapped in a small-town gym teacher's life. And now fate had dropped a real-live puzzle into her lap in the form of one sarcastic mountain of nerd. She just couldn't resist.

That being the case, she eased into the investigation.

"The first teaching assignment is rough, isn't it?" She tried to sound sympathetic instead of nosy.

His expression went from disgruntled to guarded. "Who said this was my first teaching job?"

The change in him sent a thrill through her veins. Hot on the scent of something rotten in Denmark, she answered, "I just assumed. Are you saying it isn't?"

"That's what I'm saying."

"Oh, sorry. Well, how long have you been at it? Besides the last two weeks here at DH, I mean."

"Five years."

"Almost as long as I have," she mused, and nibbled her lip. "Where'd you get your degree?"

He glanced impatiently toward the gym. "Look, class is supposed to start in five minutes. Shouldn't we—"

Yes, we should, but you're not getting off that easily. "UCLA?" she guessed quickly.

His disgusted gaze swung back to her face and sharpened. "What is this, Twenty Questions?"

"No. This is conversation. Come on, George, you can do it."

"USC," he growled.

Just like that, she got sidetracked. "Hey! Me too!"

"Is that right?"

She nodded. "Quite a coincidence, huh? We both went to USC."

"Yeah."

"And we're both gym teachers."

"Imagine that."

"Yeah. Imagine that."

Not that this was a life she'd freely chosen.

A natural athlete descended from a long line of natural athletes, Candy loved sports. Her family had expected her to follow the rest of the clan into the record books, and Lord only knew she had tried and tried again. But she never quite measured up.

She was eighteen and miserably frustrated when her problem was finally diagnosed. Denial lasted through her first disappointing year of college track and field. Eventually, the whole family had been forced to accept the facts.

Even the Johnsons had to admit that Olympic-level sports was no place for an athlete born without the killer-competitor gene. Win or lose wasn't in Candy's makeup; she just liked to play the game.

"Degree in physical education?" He nodded, and she wrinkled her nose. "Me too. It seemed like the thing to do at the time." Actually the degree had been her family's idea of a reasonable compromise. She smiled wryly. "The practical thing to do. I'm a very practical person, you know. Just ask anybody."

No one—not the family, not even her best friend, Jen Maddox—knew about Candy's Walter Mitty wild side. Insatiable curiosity combined with an active imagination and a thirst for adventure did not a happy gym teacher make.

"I'm twenty-nine years old and thinking it might be time for a career change," she muttered absently.

"You don't like teaching?"

Still talking to herself, Candy murmured, "Teaching's all right, but I wouldn't mind something a little more exciting."

Unfortunately, the *Donnerton Town Crier* had yet to run a want ad promising a career rife with danger, intrigue, and excitement. The *Crier* had yet to run those three words period, because they didn't apply to life in Donnerton. Candy had been saving for the last two years to go someplace—almost anyplace—else.

"Like what?" he said, and she blinked.

"Like what?"

"Like what kind of exciting career do you want?"

Good grief, she'd been babbling. Babbling was fine, but he was supposed to be the one doing it. She shook off the wayward urge to converse and straightened her shoulders.

"Never mind." Pretending nonchalance, she moved in for the kill. "So you've got a degree in physical education and you've been teaching for five years."

He scowled. "Isn't that what I—"

She smiled. "Then how come you don't know one piece of equipment from another?"

Perry Mason couldn't have done it better.

"Look, I grabbed the wrong bag of balls because I

wasn't paying attention, all right? Cut me some slack, would you? A couple of weeks ago I moved to a new town *and* started a new job. I've got a lot on my mind right now."

His explanation sounded entirely plausible, dammit. Because it irritated her, she decided to rattle his cage. "Maybe, but I think I'll ask Mr. Carmichael to recheck your references just the same."

She wouldn't, of course. Next to Hank Rebman the science sot, Candy was the principal's least favorite person, simply because she'd once told him to keep his pudgy pink paws to himself. In front of the entire student body. She took full credit for the hands-off call, but the audience had been Carmichael's fault.

Only an idiot tried to cop a feel in the middle of a pep rally while standing in front of an open mike.

The reference threat was a good one, but it didn't even get a rise out of Pinhead. Well, not exactly. He didn't move a muscle. His gaze grew oddly intent as he began turning the ball in his hands again, very slowly.

"Are you just naturally nosy?" he asked softly. "You know what they say about cats and curiosity, don't you, Ms. Johnson?"

All of a sudden something shimmered in the air between them. Danger, she thought, and immediately felt foolish. Still, it confused her so that she could only shake her head.

His eyebrows lifted mockingly. "You *don't* know what they say about cats and curiosity?"

He was toying with her. That realization was the prod she needed to shift right back into irritation. Her spine straightened with an almost audible snap.

"I know what they say about cats and satisfaction, George. Which is why I'm going to ask Mr. Carmichael to check you out. Today."

She *would* ask Carmichael, by God. No badly dressed greaser Adonis in generic track shoes was going to best Candy Johnson, she fumed, and strode toward the gym doors.

She smacked the bar, shoved open the door, and glared over her shoulder. "Better watch your butt, mister." The door closed behind her with a satisfying crash.

Later that night the man Candy knew as George Price ran a hand through his freshly washed hair. No oil slick, thank God. Hopefully, he'd wrap up this caper before he developed a permanent scalp condition. Sacrificing his ponytail for this role had been bad enough.

Today he'd almost blown the job. A man who lived by lies and deceit and managed to blend into some of the world's most dangerous slums had no business slipping up on something as simple as athletic equipment. Swearing softly, he admitted that today's unprecedented goof was one more sign that he was a short spark away from burnout at the ripe old age of thirty-five.

Long days and longer nights spent drifting from place to place to run one racket after another, dealing with the scum of the earth on a daily basis—it all gnawed at his soul. Young and stupid were behind him; he was way past living for the thrill. Laying it all on the line while the big boys plotted the moves, grabbed the rewards, and played it safe didn't cut it anymore. Maybe it was time to get out of the business.

Dressed in nothing but a fierce scowl, he shrugged off the useless maybe and padded through the four-room dump he called home, sweet temporary home, skirting the sorriest collection of Naugahyde and pressed wood known to man. He reached for the phone and dialed. Gebhardt answered on the first ring.

"Hey, hey, buddy! Wassup?"

"Nothing is up. Not one damned thing. It's unnatural."

"Pretty slow, huh? Well what'd you expect out there in the back end of beyond?"

"I expected to make contact. Pick up a lead. I didn't expect to be bored senseless! Only one thing happens here with any regularity, and I'm telling you, pal, a man can only watch so much grass grow. Tell me you made a mistake. Tell me I should leave for L.A."

"Uh-uh."

"Frisco?"

"Sorry, bro."

"Okay, I'm desperate. Sacramento."

"No can do."

"I'm willing to beg, Geb."

"Damn. Much as I'd like to hear you grovel, I'll have to pass. Traynor says Donnerton is the place to connect."

"Ah, hell."

"I hear you, Teach."

"And that's another thing. How come you guys couldn't put together a better front for me? Something with a little flash and style."

"Hey, we're talking small-town America here. Flash and style would stick out like a Harley in a bicycle race. We wanted you in the heart of the action, and this Nelson guy was the only local we could take out with no muss or fuss. Everybody in town knew he had a heart condition."

"Yeah, but he was a gym teacher."

"You got something against gym teachers?"

Price hesitated, thinking of Candy Johnson. Melanie Griffith pretty, with a bed-tousled cap of platinum-blond hair, pansy-blue eyes, and killer legs that stretched damn near to her armpits, the statuesque Ms. Johnson was too tempting for his own good.

In short: "Yes. Gym teachers are a pain in the butt."

"That's harsh."

"I always hated gym class."

"I knew you in high school, remember? You cut gym four years running."

"Like I said."

Geb tsk-tsked. "Okay. What happened?"

The girls' team had won, for one thing, and he'd never developed a taste for crow. All of which had nothing to do with the scam. Candy Johnson, on the other hand . . .

"We may have a problem."

Suddenly Gebhardt was all business. "What kind of problem?"

"There's this woman—"

He was interrupted by a snort. "Yeah, right. Listen, old friend, the day *you* have woman trouble will be the day I wake up with hair."

Price grinned, picturing his lean cohort's glossy dome. "Stranger things have happened."

"Not in this century, man. But we digress. You were saying?"

"I was telling you about this nosy woman I've got on my case."

"Hah. Nosy woman is redundant; all women are nosy. It's hormonal. And you being the new stud on the block, the local chicks are bound to check you out."

"*Stud?* George Price?"

Silence. "Point taken. More like dud."

"Right. Anyway, she's not man-woman curious, she's what-are-your-references-and-where-do-you-really-come-from curious."

"You want me to take care of her?"

"No, I'll do it. I have a plan."

"I knew it! Nobody does plans better than you."

"This is true."

"And you're so modest too. So how you gonna handle this lady snoop?"

From *handle* Price's mind jumped to *hands* and what his could do with Johnson's curves, a bed, and time to spare. He indulged the fantasy for one wistful second before firmly discarding it.

"I'm going to get close to her."

The pause was deafening. "How close? Man, you don't want to get tangled up with some babe and blow the gig. We need this buy or we are out of business."

"Give me some credit here. Have I ever blown a gig?"

"No, but we're talking woman now. Unpredictable

and dangerous. So I repeat, how close are you going to get?"

"I'm just going to take her out, get to know her. Give her something to think about besides my teaching credentials."

Geb didn't sound convinced. "I don't—"

"There's no other way. It isn't just the fact that she's asking a lot of questions. I haven't been able to dig up jack on Farmer. When it comes to talking to a newcomer, these folks make clams look gabby. I need an in, and Candy Johnson is it. There's just one problem."

"What's that?" Geb asked with a defeated sigh.

"The woman can't stand me."

"I've seen you as Price. I can't stand you either. So what you gonna do?"

Price smiled. "Change her mind, of course."

The suspect felt secure because Columbo looked dumb and harmless. He always looked that way when he closed in for the kill.

"Better take it on the lam, punk," Candy advised, stepping around the corner.

Her presence sent the perp scrambling under the pyracantha next to the house. Poised in his best predator's crouch, Columbo followed his prey with only a quick jerk of his head.

When the last millimeter of mouse tail whipped out of sight, the cat sat back on his haunches. Mottled tail twitching forebodingly, he slowly turned his scruffy head to pin Candy with an accusatory golden glare.

"*Mmrrow.*"

"I know. I'm scum." She scooped him into her arms and nuzzled. "But trust me, this isn't a good night to drop masticated mouse at my feet."

Clammy Hands Carmichael had nixed her request for a reference recheck, but knowing how his tiny mind worked, she hadn't been surprised. The you-obviously-have-a-problem-dealing-with-men speech, on the other hand, had come as a *complete* surprise.

"What a meathead," she muttered, unlocking the back door.

Carmichael seemed to think that her aversion to his public grope-and-grab signaled serious psychological problems, a diagnosis apparently clinched by her attitude toward the school's other resident bonehead.

"Perfectly understandable, my dear," she mimicked in a nasal whine. "As a woman working in the male-dominated field of sports, you no doubt feel threatened by men and push them away. It's very simple, really."

She plopped Columbo down and scooped food into his dish, grumbling, "I'm not going to get any backup from Carmichael. I'll have to check out Price myself."

The evidence against him was circumstantial but disturbing. Candy ticked each item off on her fingers.

"The soccer-ball snafu. He got weird when I asked him a few innocent questions about it."

Columbo stopped eating and shot her a glance.

"Right. He's *always* weird, and the questions weren't so innocent. But what about his pregame pep talk? 'Win one for the Gipper' is a pep talk. 'Kick some feminist butt' is *not* a pep talk.

"Sportsmanship?" She tossed up her hands. "Price

wouldn't know sportsmanship if it patted him on his gorgeous butt. If that man is a gym teacher, I'll eat my sports bra."

Which left the question of what he really was and how to go about finding out.

Sherlock had street urchins and Hammer had snitches. All *she* had was determination and a suspicious mind.

She could probably sneak a peek at Price's employment record, but she wouldn't know a falsified document if it was written in flashing red neon. A hacker could take Pinhead's date of birth or Social Security number and ferret out all kinds of information. Unfortunately, WordPerfect for Windows and a rudimentary knowledge of word processing wouldn't produce the same results.

That left going to the source. She gave a frustrated groan because the source usually greeted her with a nasty sneer like the one Columbo reserved for Mrs. Higgenbotham's toy schnauzer. Candy would have to get on Pinhead's good side before she could pry out his darkest secrets. Since she didn't know why he disliked her in the first place, getting on his good side wouldn't be easy.

Of course nobody ever said fighting for truth and justice would be.

TWO

This is a good idea.

Candy tried to believe it as she watched the sun glint off the windows of Donnerton's only high-rise apartment complex. Those three lofty stories had the dubious honor of housing one George Price in ground-floor apartment 1A.

There were more pleasant ways to spend a Saturday morning. She could wash socks, for example, or balance her checkbook. But her inquiring mind wanted to know about Pinhead, so she'd resigned herself to being sociable, even if the prospect made her queasy.

She'd decided to offer the hand of friendship here instead of at school, because if Price laughed in her face, she wanted to murder him in private.

Keep it light, she reminded herself as she started toward the building. *One of those I-just-happened-to-be-in-the-neighborhood-and-decided-to-bury-the-hatchet things.*

The plan was elementary. Invite Price to dinner,

render him catatonic with food and relaxation, and *shazam!*

"He'll be putty in my hands," she murmured, an image that had her absently wiping one palm on her leggings before she rang the bell. She waited and rang again.

"Keep your shirt on and your finger off the damned doorbell! I'm coming!"

Candy winced. Pinhead obviously wasn't a morning person.

"Great," she muttered with a huff. Lifting her chin, she pasted on her jauntiest smile, prepared to soothe the savage beast. The door flew open, and she found herself smile to snarl with a shirtless Price.

"What the—" His glower melted into a surprised scowl. "Oh, it's you."

"Hi," she said, as her gaze homed in on his torso. It was quite simply to die for, and she might have done just that if the burning in her lungs hadn't reminded her to breathe. Somewhere in the oxygen-starved recesses of her brain, she remembered she'd been raised by and with the physically fit. Well-ripped pecs and washboard abs were nothing new and shouldn't induce temporary paralysis.

Black hair feathered over his chest and around his flat nipples to streak down his belly and disappear under the waistband of his low-riding navy sweats. His hips were narrow, his shoulders broad and roped with muscle.

"Well? What do you want?"

Now, there was a loaded question. Candy blinked

away the idiotic reply that popped into her head and cleared her throat. "Can I come in?"

The fact that he said, "Yeah, come on in. I just made coffee," stunned her almost as much as the sight of that stellar chest had. He turned toward the kitchen but she stood riveted to the spot, staring at the world's sexiest flip side. It was sheer force of will that allowed Candy to drag her eyes away to scan her surroundings.

Cheap, stark, and impersonal, she decided, drawing a shaky breath. Kind of like a really bad hotel room. She wondered if he planned to check out anytime soon.

The smell of coffee led her to the kitchen and Pinhead, who was rummaging through the refrigerator. By the time he pulled out a pint of milk and closed the door, she'd managed a quick inventory of the contents: milk, beer, and a tub of margarine.

Ripe for the plucking. She almost rubbed her hands together in glee as she sat down at the postage-stamp table, picked up her cup, and drank.

The invitation to coffee had shocked her.

The coffee itself almost killed her.

"God," she gasped when the first sip had muscled its way down, "that stuff's lethal!"

He sampled and shrugged. "Tastes okay to me. I like my coffee strong."

"So do I, but not this strong." Industrial waste wasn't this strong.

"Cut it with milk."

There weren't enough cows in Texas. "No, that's all right. I'll just let it cool off a little."

He chuckled wickedly. "You do that." Leaning back

in his chair, he stretched out his legs and crossed his ankles. "So what can I do for you?"

You could put on a shirt, Candy thought, watching muscles flex as he reached out to toy with his cup. As soon as she realized where her eyes had strayed, again, she jerked them back to her own cup and took a punishing swig of Price's Die-Hard Drip. *Get down to business, Johnson.*

Gazing stubbornly into her coffee, she moistened her lips. "The thing is . . . uh . . . George . . ." The rest of the sentence died on the tip of her tongue, leaving a bad taste in her mouth.

"Yes?"

Taking a deep breath, she forced herself to just spit it out. "Come to dinner."

His silence had her glancing up despite her better judgment to meet his probing eyes. "Dinner?"

"Yes."

"When?"

"Tonight."

"You cook?"

"Don't look so skeptical," she muttered. "I'm no Julia Child, but I won't accidentally poison you either."

"Does that mean you'll poison me on purpose?"

The man could give lessons in obnoxious. "Of course not," she snapped.

Head tilted, he eyed her narrowly. "Why?"

"Poisoning people is against the law."

"No. Why do you want me to come to dinner all of a sudden?"

Gathering the scattered threads of her patience,

Candy said, "You and I got off on the wrong foot somehow."

"You think so?"

"Yes." *And it's all your fault.* She squelched that in favor of: "I'd like to change that."

He stared in apparent disbelief. "You would?"

"Yes."

His eyes narrowed. "Why?"

Because it's the only way I can expose you for the big phony that you are.

"Well?"

"Things will run smoother at school if we at least learn to tolerate one another, don't you think?"

"Maybe."

She hid her rekindling irritation behind a winning smile. "Sure they will. The atmosphere in the gym would be a lot more pleasant if the two of us weren't constantly at each other's throat."

His gaze dropped to her throat and lingered. "Mmm."

For some reason, she suddenly found it hard to swallow. "So what do you think?" barely made it through the constriction.

He pursed his lips and rubbed his jaw while his eyes tried to bore a hole through her skull. Candy barely resisted the urge to squirm in her chair.

She was ready to suggest they forget the whole thing when he nodded slowly. "Okay." A grudging concession that forced her to swallow a *gee, thanks.*

"Good," she said brightly, and stood. If she didn't get out of here right now, she'd brain the big jerk.

"You sure you can cook?"

"Not enthusiastically. But even I can broil a couple of steaks," she assured him through a strained smile.

He climbed to his feet, his sheer size making her feel small and delicate and agitated. In a lightning flash of self-discovery she found out that she absolutely detested feeling small and delicate and agitated.

"Steak sounds good. Shall we say six?"

All of a sudden he was way too close and much too pushy. He smelled of soap, coffee, and raw male, and she was abruptly desperate for distance. Lots of it.

"Uh . . . no," she stammered, backing out of the kitchen. He matched her retreat step for step. "I have some things to do this afternoon, and then I have to shop for food. Make it eight."

"Tell you what," he said, and stopped her dead when he reached out to run a finger under her bangs. "I'll meet you at Larson's at seven, and we'll shop together."

A touch on the forehead can't scramble your brains, she thought dizzily. "You don't have to do that." She spun away before he could touch her again and hurried through the living room.

He was right on her heels. "I want to."

Hand on the doorknob, she tossed a harassed look over her shoulder. "You do?"

"Absolutely."

Somehow the door opened and she found herself outside. "Well, if you're sure—"

"I am. See you later, Candy." He shut the door.

Her pulse couldn't possibly have leaped just because he'd used her first name. No way. She stared at the door before turning slowly to walk away, feeling unsettled and . . . well, manipulated. But why?

She'd gotten what she wanted, which was Price for dinner and questioning. The whole operation had gone according to plan. Ergo, she was in complete control.

Wasn't she?

"What are you looking at?"

"You," Candy blurted, and smiled sheepishly when Price raised an eyebrow. "You look different."

"How so?"

She shoved the ancient shopping cart down the produce aisle and shook her head. "Never mind."

Pinhead probably wouldn't appreciate the explanation about how she found it hard to believe that the man walking through Larson's with her was the same one who'd jangled her nervous system that morning.

He certainly had a way with clothes, she mused, a bad one. The brown corduroy jacket gave new meaning to the expression *worse for wear*, sagging from his broad shoulders in an exhausted slump, its pocket gaping with plastic and ballpoints. The faded jeans were all right—actually, the way they hugged his thighs was close to spectacular. Of course the buttoned-up button-down white shirt pretty much killed the effect.

The Incredible Hunk gone Nutty Professor, she decided after another sideways glance, and struggled to hide her grin.

"You're doing it again," he muttered.

"Sorry." Then, before he could try to pin down her thoughts: "How about a salad?"

He slanted her a hooded glance but nodded. "Fine. I think I'll see if I can find a good bottle of wine to go with the steak."

Candy ran her tongue over her teeth with a pointed look toward Larson's one-shelf wine selection. "A good bottle of wine?"

He followed her gaze and grimaced. "I'll settle for one without a screw-on cap."

"This is Donnerton."

"And I'm an optimist."

"Obviously."

"Oh, come on. A mediocre Burgundy isn't too much to ask, even in Donnerton."

Her eyes widened. "Mediocre Burgundy. You know wine?"

"Is that so hard to believe?"

"I've tasted your coffee."

He scowled. "There's nothing wrong with my coffee."

"Not a thing. Other than the fact that it's toxic."

"We are not talking about coffee," he growled. "We are talking about wine. I'll meet you at the checkout."

George Price had so much as an inkling about wine? Eyes narrowed, suspicions aroused by yet another kink in an already perplexing personality, Candy stared after him, thoughts whirling.

Sometime during the long afternoon it had dawned on her that this whole dinner thing had been too damned easy. Based on past experience, she'd imagined it might take weeks to lure Pinhead into her trap. Instead he'd all but pounced on her invitation.

He was up to something.

Maybe she should call it off.

By the time she'd filled the rest of her grocery list, she'd plotted a couple of worst-case scenarios, factoring in Price's IQ, which might rival that of her gym socks. After due consideration, she ignored her misgivings and wrestled her cart toward the checkout. She could handle Pinhead.

"Company for dinner tonight?"

Candy smiled wryly. Edwina Bimson didn't miss a trick. "Yep."

The cashier's little black eyes lit up. She ran a wizened finger over Candy's T-bones. "Anybody I know?"

No doubt. Edwina knew everybody *and* their business. And what Edwina knew, all Donnerton knew, usually in under an hour.

Candy scrambled for an evasive reply. She could live without the whole town knowing she was wining and dining Pinhead Price. "Uh—"

"I knew it!" Cackling madly, Edwina slapped her bony thigh. "It's Arvin, right? Hot damn!"

Candy's jaw dropped. Good God! Edwina thought the mysterious dinner guest was Arvin Carmichael! "Edwina—"

"I knew he had it in him! Somewhere," she added in a mutter. Sweeping the steaks across the scanner, she grinned jubilantly.

"I'm not having dinner with Mr. Carmichael." Not in this lifetime. Dinner with Price was bad enough.

"You're not? Aw, shoot. How come?"

Candy cleared her throat. "Well, he's . . ." How to put this delicately?

"A worm. Hell, girl, everybody knows that."

Worm didn't quite do him justice. Not when the man had all those hands, Candy remembered with a shudder. "He's—"

"Sleazy." Edwina nodded, and screwed her wrinkles into a hopeful expression. "Maybe you could overlook Arvin's little drawbacks? As a personal favor to me?"

"I'm afraid your nephew isn't my type."

"Not your type." Edwina sighed morosely. "Might as well come flat out with it, honey. That doofus Arvin ain't anybody's type. Takes after his daddy that way. Well then, who *are* you feeding tonight?"

Candy glanced at the conveyor belt, gauging her chances of holding off the inquisition. She peeked over her shoulder to check on Pinhead. Brown bag tucked under one arm, he was leafing through a magazine.

The old woman craned her neck for a look. "George Price? The new gym teacher? That's who's coming to dinner?"

Reluctantly: "Yes."

Edwina stared at Candy, then threw back her head to uncork a rusty laugh. "Well, paint me pink and call me Hatty! I'll say one thing for you, girl, when you set out to rope yourself a man, you cut out prime stock."

It was Candy's turn to stare. "I do?"

"Ohhhh, yes. Tell you what, too, if I were forty years younger I'd give you a run for your money with that one, and I'd win." Edwina sighed lustily. "Why, I'd have that big old studmuffin flat on his back faster than you could spit."

"But . . ." Surely Edwina knew? "He's a nerd. He wears a pocket protector and everything."

"A pocket protector." The cashier shot the heavens an exasperated glance before leaning across the checkout counter. "You've got to get your mind off the package and onto the beefcake, girl. Shades of Schwarzenegger, honey, that man is B-U-I-L-T. Don't tell me you haven't noticed?"

Candy turned to look at Pinhead again. "Yes, but—"

"But nothing. I guarantee you—turn off the lights and peel him out of those god-awful clothes, and you'll find yourself with a whole lot of man."

The image leaped into Candy's head before she could block it. George Price, stretched out on black silk sheets in all his naked glory. Tan. Hairy. Hard. She swallowed. *Everywhere.*

"Umm . . ." Damn, but it was hot in here! She picked up the nearest item on the conveyor belt and fanned herself.

"Yessir, that Price is one fine hunk of male pulchree-tude." Edwina straightened and plucked the broccoli from Candy's hand.

Candy came to her senses with a jerk and a blush. Good Lord! She was fanning herself with vegetables in public. Having lascivious daydreams about George Price. They committed people for less than that.

Candy paid the bill, struggling toward equilibrium. So what if imagining Pinhead naked had tripped her trigger? It didn't have anything to do with *him*, exactly, just his gorgeous body. Nobody ever said a sexual fantasy had to have personality.

Edwina gave Candy her change with a bawdy wink. "Good luck tonight, honey."

"But it's not—"

"And don't you worry. If things don't work out between you and George, Arvin will be right there waiting in the wings."

Candy scooped up her two bags and smiled weakly. "I can't tell you how relieved that makes me feel."

THREE

It had been too damned easy.

Since Johnson usually gave him the same grimace she'd give a gum wad on the sole of her Nikes, he'd thought it might take a couple days to get her alone. But here he was at her tidy brick ranch house with two bags of groceries, a mediocre bottle of wine, and a highly suspicious invite to dinner.

She was up to something.

So what? he decided with a mental snort. He'd fooled cops on three continents. He could handle one nosy, conniving gym teacher.

The house and yard looked neat and homey, just like every other cookie-cutter property on the block. *Welcome to the set of Kate the Shrew Does Suburbia*, Price thought as he followed his hostess up the walk.

Candy Johnson was quite a beautiful woman, with her blonde hair and big, dimpled smile. She was wearing a ribbed red sweater that hugged her firm breasts, stopping mid-thigh over black leggings. The whole outfit was skin-faithful, leaving just enough room for a man's imagination.

It had taken a couple of seconds for the mental gears to catch, but he'd already realized that distracting Johnson wouldn't be such a chore after all. It would, in fact, be his very great pleasure.

She glanced back at him as she opened her door and he sent her a wide smile. Her jaw went slack, her eyes glazed over, and she blinked.

"Are we going in?"

She blinked again and rubbed her upper arms. Since the temperature hovered in the mid-seventies, he doubted her new crop of goose bumps was weather-induced.

Just then her pink tongue crept out and around her lips. His libido snapped to full, quivering attention while his mind threatened to shut down completely, giving him an unpleasant jolt. This seduction was supposed to be his game, not hers.

Dangerous woman.

"Ah . . . sure." She moved through the door, standing aside so he could come in. He stepped across the threshold, passing close enough to catch her scent, and his lower body reacted predictably.

Very dangerous woman.

Being a man with a healthy respect for danger, he decided to handle this particular hazard with extreme care. But handle it he would.

She visibly pulled herself together and murmured, "Dinner will be ready in about ten minutes. Why don't you make yourself at home?" Snatching the groceries, she made for the kitchen like Little Red Riding Hood with the Big Bad Wolf on her tail.

Price knew he should snap at her heels and keep her off balance, and he would have if he hadn't been thrown off balance himself by the room she left him in.

He stared. In his imagination he stepped outside to tack a sign on the front door: SUBURBIA STOPS HERE.

A riot of color, shelves loaded with books, and plants everywhere. He hadn't seen greenery this dense since the Colombian job. He crossed to the bookshelves, read a few titles, and blinked.

Dumb jockettes didn't read G. K. Chesterton.

His agile mind was busy with the Johnson-character rewrite when a flicker of movement had him looking down.

The yellow stare belonged to a patchwork mutant hairball that might have been a cat. With the learned caution of a man who knew himself to be on the animal kingdom's Ten Most Wanted List, he froze, eyeballing his surveillant. Yeah, it was probably a cat.

Wondering when he'd become a masochist, he crouched and extended a wary hand. The unwavering feline gaze dropped to his outstretched fingers. Price shifted uncomfortably. "Well?"

"*Mmrow.*"

Call it a gap in his education, but he didn't speak tabby. When the furball started toward him, he tensed, fatalistically bracing for bloodshed, namely his. The affectionate nudge-and-rub caught him by surprise.

Unless he was seriously misreading the body language here, this scraggly quadruped liked him. Feeling ridiculously pleased, he gave the critter's head a ginger pat, which was obviously the right move, because it set the thing to purring like a well-tuned Porsche.

"Well, I'll be damned."

Things weren't going quite as planned, and Pinhead wasn't as stupid as he looked. But then nobody could be.

It was time to revise her strategy. The way to Price's mouth obviously wasn't through his stomach. Candy was beginning to think she'd need a crowbar to pry out those alleged dark secrets of his.

The man was a menace.

First he'd assaulted her with The Smile. Nerd he might be, but Price's smile packed enough near-nuclear power to vaporize every one of the two hundred bones in a woman's body. And it took those bones exactly seventeen minutes to reconstitute themselves.

A genuine menace.

Then there had been the touching little scene with her cat. If that wasn't the most underhanded, sneaky . . .

Okay, he probably hadn't known she was watching. But nobody could witness that cross-species male-bonding session—complete with Price's gosh-he-likes-me grin—without softening at least a little. Just *where* she'd gone soft was debatable, but Candy suspected brain damage.

Definitely a menace, she thought, fingers drumming on the tablecloth.

But a tight-lipped menace. So far he'd given away exactly nothing. Zip. Well, she wasn't through with him yet. Sooner or later she'd have him singing like a one-hundred-ninety-five-pound canary.

"What?"

Candy focused with a start. *Get a clue*, she ordered herself. *Any clue*. Unfortunately, the question she came up with was, "Huh?"

He leaned back in his chair. "What's on your mind?"

She frowned. "What makes you think there's anything on my mind?"

"You're looking at me like this." Leaning forward, he squinched up his eyes and stared rudely.

Oh, great. He's being observant. "Uh . . ."

"What were you thinking about?"

Interrogation. But she couldn't tell him that. So she said, "Dessert," and sprang out of her chair.

Twenty minutes and two slices of triple-fudge layer cake later, she herded Price outside. The dull yellow glow of the bug bulb slid over the sheen of his hair as he settled into her backyard swing.

There, amid the cricket chirps and random dog barks that passed for nightlife in Donnerton, Candy initiated her new plan. She'd lull Price with repetitive motion and boring conversation then slip in a few innocuously phrased but incisive questions.

She tried to concentrate on that plan as she sat next to him. It was either that or notice again how really good he smelled. Of course, it would take more than a whiff of warm musk and hot man to derail *her* train of thought, she vowed on a long, covert inhale.

"Nice night," he offered.

Quit sniffing and get down to cases. She nudged the

swing into slow motion. "Uh-huh. This is my favorite time of year." There. Seasonal talk. That was certainly boring.

"It's a nice little town."

"You think so?"

"It's okay."

"Uh-huh." If you were into tedium.

"People are nice too."

Arvin Carmichael leered in her mind's eye. "Most of them."

"How long have you lived here?"

"Six years."

"And you really like it?"

She snorted. It was automatic. "Do I look comatose?"

It was supposed to be a rhetorical question, but Price leaned in kissing close and gave her an unprovoked once-over that sent corpuscles scrambling rapidly through her veins. "Not hardly," he drawled, settling back again.

Candy flatly refused to hyperventilate. For some dumb reason her body kept reacting as if Price were Brad Pitt, and she was fed up with it. She slanted a glare at her guest.

"With any luck I'll be here for only a couple more years." Irritated by the breathy sound of her voice, she determinedly leveled it before asking, "How about you? Do you like it here?"

"Not half as much as you do."

Aha! An opening! "Then why did you come?"

Good question. Nicely phrased. Snoopy without being obvious.

He shrugged. "My last coaching job ended all of a sudden after four and a half years. Wiped out in one of those frantic, end-of-the-fiscal-year budget crunches. I needed another job, and there weren't many open two weeks before Labor Day."

Good answer. Nicely phrased. Uninformative without being evasive.

Damn!

Then she remembered why there had been a last-minute opening at Donnerton High. A quick stab of sadness diverted her from her line of questioning. "Poor Karl."

"Who?"

"Karl Nelson, the man you replaced. He had a heart attack, you know. At a Ramada in Anaheim."

"So I heard."

"He was awfully excited about winning that trip to Disneyland." Karl flew off to the Magic Kingdom wearing a tacky Hawaiian shirt; he flew home wearing a tasteful brass urn. "We never did find out what happened down there."

"That's tough."

"Yeah." Taking a deep breath, she shook off the momentary grief. "How come you began so late?" Catching his quizzical glance, she clarified. "Teaching. You're what? Thirty-four?"

"Thirty-five."

"And you've only been teaching five years?"

"So? Oh, I get it. Four years in the army, two years of diddling around before I decided to use the GI Bill. Another four years at USC."

"And your last job?"

His sigh sounded resigned. "What about it?"

"What about it?" She shook her head. "You're going to make me work for every crumb, aren't you? Where was it?"

"At a high school."

"At a high school." She rolled her eyes. "Come on, George, loosen up. We're supposed to be getting to know each other here. Don't you have at least one rollicking tale about the time you foiled the Great Girls' Locker-Room Raid?"

His lips twitched as he shook his head. "Sorry."

"I don't believe it. Teachers trade war stories. It's traditional. As storytellers we rank right behind new mothers and Edwina Bimson. You can't tell me that nothing interesting happened at this high school in—"

"L.A."

Diverted again, Candy brightened. "Really? I have a friend who teaches high school in L.A." She hadn't seen Jen in the six months since she'd married Brent Maddox. "I wonder if you know her?"

"Probably not. It's a big city."

"You might know her, because she's kind of famous. She married a millionaire. It was on TV and in all the papers. Do you know a Jennifer Mad—"

"You've got frosting on your face."

"What? I do?" Candy brushed at her left cheek. "Where?"

"Not there." For a guy who wore government-issue glasses, he had a very smooth move. All of a sudden they were almost cheek to cheek and he had her hand. In a voice two impossible octaves lower, he rumbled, "Here. I'll show you."

Later she'd decide he had no right to use her own digits against her. She'd remember how she should have told him to keep his big hands to himself, this minute, or else. Later she'd be both appalled and astonished to realize that with nothing more than a long look, Pinhead Price had turned her into a pliant zombie. She'd curse him for it. She'd curse herself.

Later.

Now, trapped in gray eyes gone smoky, she let him guide her index finger to brush the corner of her mouth. Eyes locked with hers, he then guided it into *his* mouth, swirling his tongue over each individual nerve ending while she watched.

Shouldn't chiseled lips feel . . . well, chiseled? As opposed to warm and soft? Within the hot, secret cavern of his mouth, his tongue stroked over her skin while sparks crackled up her arm.

She needed oxygen, but her lungs wouldn't work. Her heart, on the other hand, worked *too* well, pounding in deep, hard strokes. All of a sudden her mouth was dry.

Slowly, he slid her finger from between his lips, scraping it lightly with his teeth, and she quivered. Some faint internal alarm warned her that quivering was a very bad sign. She tried to break free. "I think—"

"No," he murmured, "no. Don't think." And pulling her close, he kissed her.

Oh, God, she thought, *I am in big trouble.*

This was not your standard, tentative first kiss. Not the inept kiss of a total nerd. It was a deep, scorching, incredibly *ept* kiss. This kiss set off a hormonal chain reaction and unleashed a sex-crazed monster.

And the monster was her.

She wrapped her arms around his neck, molded her mouth to his, and let him drag her deeper. Need—unfamiliar and all-consuming—slammed into her, a mountainous wave that boiled up and over. But as their tongues met and dueled she knew the kiss wasn't deep enough. No kiss could be deep enough.

Just then he slid a hand up her thigh and pulled her right leg across his lap, and she found herself straddling him. The swing rocked crazily as she settled against his erection, and they both groaned. His arms streaked around her waist and clamped her against him.

Their mouths were fused, her breasts were plastered against his brick-wall chest, and she still wasn't close enough. Her fingers speared into his hair, clenched . . . and slid.

Operating in high sex drive, her body screamed, *Hold that call.* Her brain said, *Hello?* and screeched a full-stop order. Candy shrieked and scrambled off his lap.

Standing a good five feet away, cloaked in horrified dismay and heavy breathing, she gaped at him. Good heavens! She'd let George Price kiss her crazy! She was losing her mind!

He stood and stepped toward her. Candy leveled a greasy finger. "You stay away from me, you menace!"

Price stopped, his expression a pitiful attempt at injured innocence. He was too big and obviously turned on to do injured innocence well. "What's wrong?"

The man had just kissed her into a terminal state of lust and he wanted to know what was wrong. Okay, she could do one of three things: She could jump his bones. She could strangle him. Or: "Go home."

He stared. "What?"

"You have to go home."

"Now?"

"If not sooner."

His voice dropped to that seductive purr she belatedly recognized as risky business. "Are you sure?"

No! cried her needy body. "Absolutely, positively," said her mouth.

Head tilted, he eyed her speculatively. Candy braced, half expecting him to pounce, half hoping he would, although she wasn't sure what she'd do to him if he did. It seemed to be a toss-up between a roundhouse and ravishment. Her circuits were still badly jumbled.

Then he walloped her with The Smile, and those circuits sizzled, popped, and blew.

"I'll go," he said. "For now."

He stalked off into the darkness, trailing testosterone, while Candy shivered in his wake. A single thought drifted through the wreckage of her peace of mind. *Uh-oh.*

He'd wanted only to deflect her prying, but damned if that blonde bombshell hadn't exploded in his face. Worse yet, he was the fool who'd blithely lit her fuse. The fact that he couldn't wait to do it again hinted at a previously undiscovered appetite for self-destruction.

But what a way to go!

Price cut off the water. Teeth chattering, he

climbed out of the shower, snagged a towel to blot ice water off his chest, and rehashed the list of excellent reasons for avoiding Candy Johnson like the bubonic plague.

First off, he wasn't sure he liked her. Okay, so tonight she'd shown him her polite, sociable, friendly side. She'd also shown him her nosy and pit-bull-tenacious side.

He was a man involved in shady dealing; the last thing he needed was a bad case of the hots for a leggy busybody who wouldn't know a stone wall if she ran headfirst into it.

Slinging the towel around his neck, he ambled into the bedroom telling himself to think about the scam. He had to sew this one up. Johnson was curious enough, and stubborn enough, to unravel it down to the last thread. The kind of news that could generate was generally limited to the obituaries.

This gig could get seriously hairy; he had to keep a clear head. Kissing Johnson destroyed synapses he couldn't afford to lose. Falling into bed with her would probably give him the equivalent of a full frontal lobotomy.

Oh, yeah. There were plenty of arguments for steering well clear of her, and only two reasons not to.

He needed information. Farmer wasn't exactly strolling down the sidewalks of Podunk to chew the fat with the locals. He hadn't shown his face in two months. Price was tired of sitting around and getting nowhere.

The buy would go down sometime during the next few weeks. If he meant to be in on the action, he needed Farmer. He had to get on the insider's track here in Dog Patch, and Johnson was his ticket to ride.

He stretched out on the bed, stacked his hands behind his head, and faced the other argument for proximity. Namely, he wanted the woman until his teeth ached.

He supposed it finally boiled down to that. She was a craving in his blood that burned frenzy-bright. He looked down at his body not knowing whether to groan or curse, because he was hard again.

There was a simple explanation for the Johnson effect, of course. A man would have to be made of stone to resist a sexy woman, especially one he knew he could drive wild with a single kiss. Price wasn't made of stone, and he didn't want to resist. Life on the edge had taught him to take his pleasure when and where he found it.

These days he was a *carpe diem* kind of guy.

Unfortunately, pleasure with Candy Johnson would have to wait. The logic was simple: If Price didn't keep his mind out from between the sheets and on the business at hand, there was an outside chance neither one of them would live long enough to regret it.

FOUR

"You know," Candy mused, "I can't quite figure out how you got me into this position."

Price tipped back his head to angle a look through the branches. She was up in a tree, straddling a limb, one black sneaker swinging lazily.

Running an appreciative eye down her long, denim-clad legs, he leered cheerfully. "Don't you remember? You put one foot on the trunk, and I put my hand on your—"

He managed to dodge the first red delicious she fired, but the second beaned him. "Ouch!"

Batting her eyelashes, she smiled sweetly. "Careful, George."

"Hey, lady, you don't scare me. You throw like a girl."

Her eyes narrowed dangerously. "Why don't you climb up here and say that?"

He chuckled and bent to scoop up her ammunition,

dropping it into his burlap bag. "Sorry, I don't climb trees."

"Since you were a kid, you mean. Same here. I haven't—"

"Since ever." His next glance found her gaping down at him, so he lifted a hand and waggled his fingers. "Come on, Johnson, let's have them."

Obligingly, she reached for an apple, but her eyes darted back to his face. "Never?"

"Nope."

"Oh, come on. Every kid climbs at least one tree." Head cocked, she peered at him. "You *were* a kid once, right?"

That section of Memory Lane was a stretch he didn't travel, even in his own mind. "No."

Judging from her stare, she didn't know quite what to make of his answer. "Figures," she muttered after a second or two, dropped the apple, and searched around for another.

There were times, he conceded ruefully as he caught and bagged the next few apples, when the truth threw up a better smoke screen than the best-laid lie.

"I was a tomboy myself. Of course trying to keep up with two brothers will do that to a girl."

"You have two brothers?"

"Yep. Both older. I was the baby and known far and wide as a champion tree climber." Then she muttered something about how her family should be happy she had at least one claim to fame.

"Your family wanted you to be famous?"

"My family wanted me to be—never mind. It's all water under the bridge."

Because she sounded embarrassed, he let it pass. But not by much. "You don't get along with your family?"

"Sure. They may be disappointed in me, but they love me."

Because she continued to mutter to herself, he called out, "Cheer up, we're almost done."

"Said the guy on the ground to the schmuck in the tree."

"Stop griping, woman. Those branches wouldn't hold me anyway."

She braced a hand on the branch above her, leaned over, and eyed him judiciously. "Hmm. Good point." Scooting farther out, she asked, "Who elected us orchard poachers, by the way? Mrs. Goldbaum has a shotgun, you know."

"It's our job, and she offered."

Branches shifted as she climbed higher. "Our job?"

"Chief decorating flunkies for the Solid Gold Harvest Dance."

"Now, that's funny." Her tone had him looking up again. Sitting on one branch with her feet planted on the one below, she had one arm wrapped around the tree trunk and a softball-sized apple in her bobbing hand. "I don't remember volunteering for that particular committee."

Recognizing the gleam in her eye, he took a wary step back. "That's okay, I volunteered for both of us."

"Uh-huh. Why?"

Because the Goldbaum orchard borders directly on Farmer's acreage. "It seemed like the school-spirited thing to do."

"George." She shook her head gravely. "Didn't anybody ever tell you that you should never volunteer?" She grinned and lobbed him the fruit. "I volunteered us to chaperon."

"Hey, no problem." He bent to jiggle his bag as if to redistribute the load, using the action to hide a grimace. So much for his Saturday-evening seduction plans.

"No problem? I said chaperon, George. That means you and I versus a couple hundred oversexed adolescents with no good on their minds."

"So what's the big deal? We make sure the kids on the dance floor keep their hands visible at all times, and keep the rest out of dark hallways, parked cars, and trouble. No sweat."

"No sweat? Are you sure you've done this before?" She sounded distinctly skeptical.

Price shook his head. It would make things a lot easier if Johnson were slower on the draw, a little less suspicious, and a lot more enthralled.

A small commotion broke out in the branches overhead. "Damn! Uh, George . . ."

"Come on down, Ms. Monkey. We've got a full load."

Leaves rustled fitfully. "I can't tell you how glad I am to hear that."

The frantic note in her voice caught his attention. A couple of quick steps brought him to the base of the tree. He glanced up. She was scrambling down at warp speed. "Something wrong?"

"Ants."

"Ants?"

"Oh, yeah. Big ones."

The reckless speed of her descent had him lifting his hands and bracing to catch her. "Be careful, dammit! It would be pretty stupid to break your neck over a few lousy ants."

"Easy for you to say," she snapped breathlessly. "You're not the one they're—"

Her sentence ended with a yelp as one hand flew off the tree to swat at her back. Not the smartest move, given her downward momentum; her torso twisted, her foot slipped, and she went into free fall.

Luck was with her, because it was a short, clear drop. Luck was with him, too, because she landed in his arms. He had a split second to enjoy the press of sleek, scented curves before she struggled to her feet and started flailing at her back.

"Don't just stand there! Get them off of me!"

Figuring he could swallow the laugh or die, Price cleared his throat. "Right."

He grabbed her by the shoulders, turned her around, and jerked the tail of her pink, long-sleeved T-shirt out of her jeans and up to her shoulders. He spotted five black ants, two on a zigzag course above her bra, two just below, and one headed south.

"Hold on," he said, and brushed them off. "There. Looks like one of them bit you." He rubbed his index finger over the pinpoint of red between her shoulder blades.

"I'll put something on it when I get home," she murmured. Then she shivered, and he froze.

Birds twittered cheerfully, filling the silence that

spun out between them as his focus shifted, almost the way a camera's does when a lens setting changes.

For the first time he registered the satiny skin under his fingertip and the graceful arch of her spine. Laying a second finger alongside the first, he slowly traced the delicate furrow of her back, stopping at the waistband of her jeans.

His imagination kept right on going.

"Do not," Candy warned shakily, "do what you're thinking about doing."

"Hmm?"

She tried to move away. He put a hand on her arm and turned her to face him.

"I mean it, George." But eyes gone dark blue homed in on his mouth and her lips parted.

"Okay," he said agreeably, and kissed her.

Her mouth was soft and warm and tasted of the apple she'd eaten earlier. The fingers wrapped around her arm tensed as his tongue dipped between her lips. He wanted to plunder her mouth, pull her to him, wrap her in his arms, bind her body to his. He didn't dare. Because if he did, if she caught fire in his arms again and let that long, curvy body melt against him, he'd take her.

But he had work to do, and dusk wasn't far off.

So he kept the kiss light, nibbling at the corners of her mouth and teasing her with his tongue. He sampled when he wanted to devour, held her in an easy grip when he ached to lay her down in the sweet-smelling grass and let her take him inside. Make him forget. Farmer, the scam, all the lies. Everything.

Shaken by the depth of a need he hadn't suspected,

didn't understand, and didn't want, he lifted his head, holding her at arm's length. She didn't look like any man's downfall. She looked dazed and well kissed, and he wanted to throw back his head and howl because he couldn't have her. Not yet. Not ever, if he had any common sense at all.

But then common sense had never been his strong point. If it had been, he'd have found another way to make a living years ago. He dropped his hand and watched Candy retreat a step as she reached back to tuck in her shirt, the action pulling the material taut over her breasts.

To hell with common sense. I'll take my chances.

After composing herself, she propped her hands on her hips and gave him a narrow, gunslinger's glare. "Didn't I tell you not to do what you were thinking about doing?"

"I didn't."

She blinked. "You didn't?"

He smiled slowly, let his heated gaze pour over her, then looked her straight in the eye. "Nope."

She fell back another step with a breathless laugh. "Then it's a damned good thing I can't read your mind, pal."

"Well," he drawled, grabbing the burlap bag with one hand and her hand with the other, "I'd be more than happy to spell things out for you."

"Forget it, George. I'm not interested in your wildest dreams." But her fingers twined with his as they walked back through the trees toward his Jeep.

❖———————❖

"What's wrong?" Candy asked when George swung the Jeep onto the shoulder less than ten minutes later.

"Nothing."

"Then why are we stopping?"

"Cornstalks."

She glanced at the wall of cornstalks alongside the road. "What about them?"

He reached over to flip open the glove compartment and extract a wicked-looking knife. "I'm going to cut some. They'll make great decorations."

"You really take this decorating-committee stuff seriously, don't you?"

"Hey, you know what they say about any job worth doing."

"Uh-huh. All right, Rambo," she said with a sigh, and unsnapped her seat belt, "let's go."

"Rambo? Oh, the knife. Hold it." He dropped a hand on her left thigh just as she swung the other leg out, and her heart bobbled giddily. "You wait here. I'll get the stalks."

"It'll go faster with two of us working, and I want to get done and head home. Thank God it's Friday." Actually, she wanted his hand off her thigh and her heart rate back where it belonged. "Come on."

When she would have shifted away, the grip on her leg tightened. "I've only got one knife."

"And it's a killer." Did he tense? She turned to look at him, but his be-reasonable expression hadn't changed. "So you cut and I'll carry."

The fingers pressed against the inside of her thigh relaxed, and she breathed a silent sigh of relief. Premature, because the fingers started to move, doing a quick change from restraint to seduction.

"Stay here, baby," he said. "You did your share of the grunt work. Let me do mine."

Heat ribboned up and out, unfurling under the slow, rhythmic stroke of his fingers. "But—"

He leaned across the gearshift to drop a soft kiss on her lips. Just coincidentally, of course, his hand inched higher. He gave her the beguiling version of The Smile. "Wait here, okay?" Then he was gone.

"Excellent idea," she murmured, running shaky fingers through her hair. "My legs probably wouldn't hold me anyway, and a little break from George will do the old cardiovascular system a world of good." It hadn't completely recovered from that scene in the orchard.

If the past few days were anything to go by, he'd taken last week's incendiary encounter as a license to touch at will, stroking the occasional index finger down her cheek or tucking a "casual" hand at the small of her back. Now that they were alone—for the first time in almost a week—he was making free with her mouth. What she couldn't figure out was why she was letting him get away with it.

The truth didn't make sense, but she recognized it just the same. George Price, poster boy for nerds everywhere, was a red-hot love affair just waiting to happen. Well, she thought, crossing her arms, he wasn't going to happen to her.

She stretched out her legs, leaned her head against the seat, and closed her eyes. Pinhead was proving quite the puzzle, only none of the pieces fit. How did the hunk in awkward clothing fit in with the man who knew his wines and carried a knife big enough to fell a redwood? Where did the irritating Pinhead come up with a dangerously tempting streak of Casanova?

The subtle, lightning-quick personality changes bothered her. Or maybe she was reading too much into them. Good Lord, even Arvin Carmichael had more than one facet to his personality. Well, probably. Still, she couldn't help feeling Price's character switches weren't natural. There was something slick and convenient, almost premeditated about them.

The man had more faces than a pinochle deck, she brooded, skirting the edges of a doze.

There was no footstep, no warning rustle of cornstalks. Just the sudden, unexpected sound of his voice. "Ready to go?"

Candy started, her eyes flew open. She straightened slowly in her seat. George strode around the Jeep and deposited what looked to be half an acre of cornstalks in the backseat while she dealt with the inexplicable conviction that he radiated an almost savage satisfaction.

"What happened?" she asked.

"What happened?" He climbed in and started the Jeep. "I got the goods, that's all. How about we stop for a bite to eat on the way back?"

Her eyes narrowed. *Got the goods.* There was something about the way he said it. . . .

When she didn't answer, he turned to look at her. "Candy?"

Stunned by what she saw in his eyes, she barely

heard her own faint answer. "Sure." She swallowed and glanced away. "Something to eat."

Oh God, his eyes . . .

The danger, intrigue, and excitement she'd never expected to find in Donnerton blazed laser-bright behind the lenses of Pinhead's glasses. The discovery left her dazed and disoriented, and reawakened her suspicions.

Unfortunately, those suspicions contained a new element: unwilling, obsessive fascination.

The dimly lit gym throbbed with bass and bodies as the Fab Four's multidecibel invitation to twist and shout blared through the speakers bracketing the table in the back corner. Surrounded by a gaggle of pumpkins and baskets of apples against a backdrop of cornstalks, the long-haired deejay in overalls and tie-dyed T-shirt looked like head produce salesman for a hippie commune.

The irony, Price mused, as his gaze wandered back to the cornstalks and his memory to the field, was incredible.

"The next one should be the last, thank God." Candy's remark was delivered in a near yell, but even though he bent close, Price barely caught it.

He nodded. Thank God was right. Four hours of crowbar duty—prying kids out of dark corners, smoky bathrooms, and hot clinches—were enough for any man. Especially for a man who was itching to get into some clinches of his own, he thought, slanting a glance at his co-chaperon.

Her bright blue dress was nothing fancy, just a simple, sleeveless sheath with a scoop neck. It wasn't tight, low-cut, or particularly short, so she shouldn't look outrageously sexy, but it skimmed a figure ripe for skimming, and the color matched her eyes. In deference to the gym floor, shoes had been left at the door, so she was in her stocking feet, and word association was driving him crazy. Words like *taking off shoes* led to *taking off stockings*, which led to taking off all kinds of other things.

She made his mouth water.

Price's lips twisted wryly. No wonder dark corners were at a premium tonight—sock hops were rocket fuel for the male libido.

The deejay's voice slid in on the last beat. "Time is, time was, time will be, my friends, and ours has just about run out. We're going to close our musical trip through the sixties and seventies with something soft and soulful, so grab your lady and hold her close for the Righteous Brothers. Until we meet again, peace, love, and togetherness."

The first haunting strains of "Unchained Melody" drifted into the gym.

Price glanced at Candy and found himself unable to look away, riveted by the rhythmic sway of her hips and her dreamy smile as she mouthed the lyrics. Her loosely folded arms reminded him of a lover's embrace. The sudden, desperate need to touch her almost brought him to his knees.

A deep breath didn't kill the need. Reminders about the wrong time and place didn't kill the need. So he leaned down, put his mouth next to her ear, and said, "Dance with me."

She went dead still, staring straight ahead. He read her lips. "We can't."

Crooking a finger under her chin, he urged her to face him. The regret and longing in her eyes were all the advantage he needed. He pressed it. "Why not?"

Rising on tiptoe, she spoke close to his ear. "School rules. Carmichael would have a fit."

He might have left it at that, but her breast was nestled against his arm. "To hell with Carmichael and his rules," he growled, grabbed her hand, and towed her through the nearest door.

The area behind the gym was cool and grassy, lit by the faint, silver wash of moonlight and the colored lights from inside. The music, muted by doors and walls, seemed distant and dreamlike. He pulled her close and enfolded her in his arms, smiling slightly when he heard her sigh. Exasperation or satisfaction? It didn't matter.

She looked up at him and shook her head. "What am I going to do with you?" But her arms crept around his waist as they started what amounted to nothing more than a slow shuffle.

"Dance."

"But the rules—"

"I'm not much on rules," he admitted, and wondered briefly what the boss would say about the understatement. A colorful string of four-letter words came to mind.

"Me either, but Carmichael will have a fit."

"I'll handle Carmichael."

"Think you're tough enough?"

If she only knew. "I'll manage."

"Uh-huh. I might have believed that after the way you bullied me into accepting a ride from you tonight. But that was before I caught you having that guy chat with my cat while you waited for me."

"I don't know what you're talking about."

"Right. I saw you, remember? Sprawled on the sofa with Columbo perched on your chest while you watched the Cowboys–Patriots game. You were discussing the weaknesses in the New England defense."

Thoroughly embarrassed because it was true, he muttered, "You talk too much. Now come here, woman." He gathered her flush against him, smiling when her head came to rest on his shoulder. "That's better."

They were molded together from chest to thigh, his wrists crossed at the small of her back, his fingertips brushing the curve of her buttocks. Her breasts pillowed against his sternum, their legs brushed as they moved. The fit, he mused as his eyes closed, was damn near perfect. And somehow, for the moment, just holding her was enough.

"I love this song," she said, and hummed along.

"Yeah, it's a classic." He angled his head, inhaling her light, sultry scent. His lips grazed her hair. "They were all classics tonight. The kids loved it."

He held her close when the song ended, leaning down to touch her lips with his. When she finally stepped out of his arms, her smile had gone shaky around the edges. "Time to get back to work."

"Yeah." He shoved his hands into his pockets, because he wanted nothing more than to grab and hold her. He tipped his head toward the doors. "You go on inside, I'll stroll around front and pull hall duty."

"Okay."

"Candy." She paused to look over her shoulder, one slender hand resting on the bar that opened the door. "Have dinner with me tomorrow night." Then, before she could voice the refusal dawning in her eyes: "Please."

She studied his face while her teeth worried her bottom lip. "All right," she said finally, and pushed into the gym, propping open the door behind her.

By the time he reached the front doors, students were surging through in an energetic wave, laughing and chatting as they streamed around him. Their calls of " 'Night, Coach," were returned absently as Price grappled with the ridiculous idea that if he wasn't careful, hanging on to a certain inquisitive, small-town gym teacher could get to be a habit.

FIVE

"Those two have the hots for each other, Gerty, you mark my words."

"The *hots* for each other? Good gravy, Edwina! What kind of gutter talk is that? The hots for each other." Pause. "Do they *really*?"

The dental-floss special in aisle four couldn't compete with the wholesale gossip over in aisle three. Candy paused in her debate between waxed and unwaxed, a half smile on her lips, curious in spite of herself.

"Well, 'course they do. You ever seen the way he looks at her?"

"No," said Gertrude Farmer. "How does he look at her?"

"Like this."

"Oh." Gerty sounded faint. "Oh, my."

"Exactly."

"I heard tell they've been spending a lot of time together after school for the last two weeks."

Candy's smile turned sympathetic. Small towns were to teenage lovers what the *National Enquirer* was to Charles and Di.

"Well, I heard more." The dramatic pause undoubtedly gave Edwina a chance to glance around cautiously before adding, "He's been seen coming out of her house. Four times. Late."

"Four times. Late. Oh, Edwina, are you sure?"

"Well, 'course I'm sure," snapped Edwina. "You don't think I go 'round spreading rumors, do you?"

"No, of course not. It's just that I—"

"Darla Winston told me, and she ought to know. She lives right next door to the woman."

Candy's smile collapsed. Darla Winston was *her* neighbor.

"Well, then."

"They're hot for each other, all right. Looks like the girl took my advice after all."

"What advice?"

As a blush surged into her cheeks Candy's lips formed a soundless *oh, no*.

"I told her . . ." Edwina's voice dropped to a whisper.

"Merciful heavens!" Gerty giggled like a schoolgirl. "Flat on his—Edwina Bimson, that's shameless! Absolutely shameless."

"Hah! Worked, didn't it?"

Gerty gasped. "You mean, you think she's—"

"Besotted. Girl's gone and got herself besotted, that's what I think. You know, Gert, I kind of had my eye on her for Arvin, but . . ." Edwina's voice faded as the two women moved down the aisle.

Still blushing, Candy ran her tongue over her teeth. Okay, things could be worse. Abject embarrassment wasn't so bad. Granted, blissful ignorance was more comfortable, but *somebody* had to be grist for the gossip mill, right? So what if everybody thought she and Price had a thing going?

She rolled her eyes. Oh, they had a thing going. She just wasn't sure what.

Against her better judgment, she'd started to like the man. George was pretty good company when he didn't have his heart set on being obnoxious. He had an irreverent sense of humor and great taste in music. He read Lawrence Sanders. And you had to like a man who talked sports with your cat.

Like she could understand. She could handle like. The growing fascination was harder to explain. How on earth had she managed to get fascinated by a man who greased his hair and looked at the world through Coke bottles?

And how had that first dinner at her house expanded into dinner almost every night since? Not to mention that picnic in Mrs. Goldbaum's apple orchard and two trips to the movies. Why didn't she just say no to George?

It was probably those mysterious undercurrents of his. They usually hummed just beneath the surface, but once in a while she glimpsed them in his eyes. A subtle alertness. Charged, expectant readiness. Razor-sharp intelligence.

George wasn't as ineffectual and oblivious as he looked.

It was just her bad luck that she was a sucker for

undercurrents. Candy huffed. Geez! The trouble a woman got into conducting one measly investigation!

Her frown deepened as she tossed a dozen eggs into her basket then absently dropped a gallon of milk in on top of them. Her observations led to one of two inescapable conclusions. Either George was a master of deception . . . or she was paranoid.

No, she couldn't be paranoid. Paranoia and rampant lust would be too much for one nervous system. Damn the man!

She'd finally caught on to his kiss-and-run MO. The process went something like this: Candy probes delicately. George gives her some prosaic, but unsatisfying answer. Candy probes deeper. George expands his answer. Candy probes doggedly. George grabs her and kisses her senseless.

She couldn't decide which she resented more—the bizarre fact that George Price *could* kiss her senseless, or the fact that he didn't do more than that.

Smiling grimly, she shook her head. "I'm way past paranoid. I'm crazy."

Edwina's laugh cackled down the aisle, and Candy winced. Donnerton's answer to the Associated Press was doubtless in full-transmission mode. Candy reluctantly angled her cart toward the checkout counter.

Somewhere between the maple syrup and the cereal, realization popped into her head, dragging a guilty blush in its wake. Edwina was wrong . . . and she was right. Candy liked George, but she was not besotted with him.

She was, however, hot for him.

And getting hotter.

———◈———————◈———

The gray mouse stood five-ten and wore a red derby. Tail draped over one arm, he jotted down their order. "Okay, that's a large, extra cheese, olives, and mushrooms. What'll you have to drink?"

"Beer." Price eyed the dinner-plate ears and foot-long whiskers.

"Sorry, sir, no alcoholic beverages. This is a family place, you know." The explanation was offered mouse to man, somewhat apologetically.

"Iced tea, then." George peered into six-inch baby blues. "That you, Carlson?"

"Yessir."

"You're a rat, Carlson."

"No, sir." Seventeen-year-old Mike Carlson ran a gloved hand over the brass buttons on his natty red vest and squared his shoulders. "I'm Charlie Cheddar."

"Ah . . . right. Sorry."

"No problem." Carlson's snout swiveled toward Candy. "How 'bout you, Ms. Johnson? What would you like to drink?"

"Oh, I'll have the same, I guess."

"Check. I'll be right back with your drinks." Turning on his paw, Charlie waded into the maze of tables, picking up kids along the way. They glommed onto his legs like a pack of squealing leeches.

"He's got guts," mused Price, and looked at Candy. "You wouldn't catch me dressed in a goofy outfit like that."

She ran her gaze over him slowly before lifting her eyes to meet his. "Of course not," she agreed solemnly, and turned to watch the kids playing video games just behind their booth.

Jaw clenched, he pretended to watch too. But he didn't see the gaudy flash of multicolored lights in Charlie Cheddar's Family Fun and Pizza Emporium. He didn't hear the tinny ragtime piano or the chattering horde. He was too busy planning Geb's payback for this stint as a fashion nightmare.

He glanced at Candy. Unlike everybody else, she hadn't swallowed his geek routine, but he was damned if he could figure out why. He had a more detailed bio than the Queen of England. The school district bought it, the state bought it. Hell, the FBI would buy it.

Not Candy. She had more questions than the White House press corps.

There was no way she'd be able to make him. He didn't have to worry about whether or not she believed his song and dance, because she was neither a major player nor a serious threat; she was a very sexy fly in his personal ointment.

Maybe he was losing his touch. Christ only knew he was tired enough. He had one of the best reps in the business, but the lies came harder these days, and life as one fictional character after another was wearing thin. Still, he was in a world of hurt if he couldn't snow one small-town gym teacher.

Of course the gym teacher in question had the instincts of a well-seasoned pro and was sharper than most cops he'd run into. What she lacked in know-how, she more than made up for in skepticism, sneakiness, and stubbornness.

She'd get this Samantha Spade look in her eye, and

he'd know he was in for it. The only way to throw her off track was to shut down that busy brain by turning on that great body.

The flaw in Plan B was that whenever he kissed her, Candy went off like a Roman candle, and he tended to ignite right along with her. His control was going fast.

"Oh, no."

His unfocused stare focused. Candy's dismayed expression had him turning to look just as a plump matron trundled through the restaurant door, towing a cute little girl by the hand. His eyes narrowed on the newcomer. *About damned time.*

She was over sixty, built like a marshmallow, and dressed like somebody's great-aunt Agnes, right down to the brogans and support hose.

He already knew the answer but asked anyway. "Who is she?"

"Gerty Farmer, professional gossip." Candy groaned, "Oh, hell! She's seen us!"

"So?"

"You don't understand."

No, but he was going to. He flicked a glance at Candy. "Calm down," he muttered while his mind raced.

A professional gossip. Professional gossips were genetically incapable of keeping their mouths shut. His first real break had been two months coming, but it looked like a doozy.

"Calm down. Right. Come here, you." Leaning across the table, Candy grabbed a fistful of his shirt and jerked.

Nose to nose, he realized she was upset. "What's wrong?"

"She's coming over here!"

"You don't like her?"

"Of course I like her!"

"Then why don't you—"

"Listen," she muttered urgently, "I overheard Edwina Bimson today."

"Bimson? You mean the lady who works at Larson's Market?"

"Yes. They were talking about our thing."

"Our thing?"

Candy peeked around his shoulder and gasped. "She's almost here!" The grip on his shirt went white-knuckle tight. "They think we're an item, okay? Everybody in town thinks we're an item."

"An item. Got it." In other words, the whole town thought Candy Johnson was his woman. Surprise was closely followed by pure satisfaction. He masked the former and tried not to worry about the latter. "So?"

"So, don't say anything that—" She snatched back her hand and popped straight in her seat, plastering on a phony smile. "Hi, Gerty."

"Evenin', Candy." Gertrude Farmer smiled and nodded, then turned brown eyes bright with curiosity his way. "Evenin'."

"Oh, I'm sorry." Candy smiled with all the sincerity of an embezzler caught with her hand in the till. "You two haven't met, have you? Gerty, this is my . . . uh, friend, George Price. George, Gerty Farmer."

"Nice to meet you, Gerty."

"Meet me too." The tyke was all chestnut curls and hazel eyes. "I'm Sara, and I'm almost exac'ly five."

"Hi, Sara."

"Here are your drinks, Coach."

Sara's head dropped back on her shoulders as she gazed up at Charlie in obvious adulation. "Hi, Charlie," she breathed.

"Hiya, kid." Charlie ruffled her ringlets. "How's it goin'?"

"I'm almost exac'ly five."

"Hey, that's swell." The mouse gave her shoulder a fraternal pat then wheeled toward the kitchen with the businesslike air of a rodent whose work was never done.

Gerty Farmer tugged on Sara's hand. "Well, we'd best be getting along now. We just wanted to stop by and say hello."

Candy looked relieved. "It was good to see you," she said, just as Sara said, "But, Gramma—" and Price said, "Why don't you join us?"

After which Candy hauled off and kicked him a good one under the table.

"We wouldn't want to impose." Judging by the avid gleam in Gerty's eye, this was a token protest at best.

Candy did a cheap imitation of disappointment. "Well, if you're sure—"

"It's no imposition," he interrupted, and caught another Nike to the shin. "Really." His eyes flashed Candy a warning: *Keep your mouth shut and your feet to yourself.* "We'll have plenty to go around."

"Can we, Gramma? Can we?"

"Well, I don't know. . . ." Gerty paused, and they

all pretended to believe she was thinking it over. Finally, she nodded briskly. "All right."

A quick seat reshuffle ended with Candy and him facing Sara and her grandmother across the booth. "There now." Gerty smoothed the flowered dress over her ample lap. "Isn't this cozy?"

"Very cozy." Candy smiled, reached down, and pinched his thigh. Really hard.

God, she was vicious! He grabbed her hand and trapped it against his leg, wondering since when did vicious women turn him on. Under the table he turned her hand and started to brush lazy circles on her palm with his thumb, swallowing a chuckle when she stiffened. "Do you like pizza, Sara?"

"Not very much."

"No? Then why did you pick this place to eat?"

"I like Charlie Cheddar *very* much."

"Is that right?" He glanced at Candy; her cheeks were flushed and the pulse in her throat raced like a rabbit.

"Yes. I'm going to marry Charlie Cheddar." Sara sighed dreamily and scrunched up her shoulders. "I'll be Mrs. Sara Charlie Cheddar and live in a big hole in the wall."

"That sounds like fun," he said, sweeping his thumb up the inside of Candy's wrist. She shivered visibly and jerked her hand away. Hiding an evil smile, Price picked up his glass.

Gerty eyed her solicitously. "Is something wrong, dear?"

"Uh—" said Candy.

"Yeah," he said, "is something wrong?"

"Not a thing," she assured them brightly, but there was the promise of retribution in her eyes as her gaze shifted past him. "Here comes our pizza."

Adoring eyes glued to the pizza-packing mouse who'd just reached their table, Sara sighed, "Hi, Charlie."

"Hiya, kid." Charlie deftly slid the pizza onto the table.

Taking advantage of the diversion, Candy leaned close and muttered in Price's ear. "Watch it, mister."

"What do you mean?"

"Thanks for the pizza, Charlie," Sara crooned.

"Hey, no problem. See ya around, kid."

"You know damn well what I mean."

Price knew he should get down to business, but it had been a long time since he'd had this much fun. According to Geb, he could charm the pharaohs' secrets out of the Sphinx herself. It wouldn't take but a few minutes to coax the family tree out of Gossipy Gerty.

"Just behave." Candy picked up a napkin and fanned her brightly burning cheeks.

Gerty caught the action. "Are you sure you're all right?"

At which point Sara piped up with, "Don'cha 'member, Gramma? Today at Larson's, Miz Bimson said Miss Candy had the hots. I heard you tell Mama."

"Sara Jane!" Gerty darted a hunted glance across the booth.

"Oh, no," Candy groaned, and dropped her head to the table.

Price grinned down at her. "Does that mean you *don't* have the hots?"

Fifty years from now she'd be old and gray and keep her teeth in a glass by the bed. She'd reminisce about the Worst Day of Her Life and laugh, Candy consoled herself. She'd overcome the base urges to gag little Sara and muzzle gossipy old ladies, as well as the perfectly understandable urge to shake George until his teeth rattled.

One day, the Worst Day of Her Life would be history.

Unfortunately, she had to live it first.

"Hi, Charlie," said Sara once again.

"Hiya, kid. Here's your lemonade."

"Oh, thank you, Charlie."

Drawn out of her brooding, Candy looked up to see Sara give the mouse the business. Charlie didn't know it, but he was being courted. So far Sara's hints that she was of marriageable age had gone right over his derby.

"No problem, kid. Everything okay here, Coach?"

"Fine, Carls—" George broke off with a quick glance at Sara. "Fine, Charlie, just fine. You do good work."

Charlie preened. "Thanks. Well, let me know if you need anything else."

"Bye, Charlie."

"See ya around, kid."

Sara gazed after Charlie, her expression two parts unrequited puppy love, three parts steely determination. "I really am gonna marry that mouse."

George chuckle-coughed into his hand. "Is Sara your only grandchild, Gerty?"

Beaming fondly, Gerty patted Sara's curly head. "Yes, she is."

"I was an only child myself," murmured George, then paused. He seemed surprised and maybe embarrassed that he'd revealed something so personal. His shrug was endearingly self-conscious. "Having a bunch of friends to play with isn't quite the same as having a brother or sister."

Eyes brimming with understanding, Gerty shook her head. "Sara doesn't have many friends her age. I know how lonely she gets—my Alice was an only child too. Harry always wanted more, God rest his soul, but it just wasn't meant to be."

"And Harry didn't come from a big family either?"

"No. He did have a brother, but Tom died in a hunting accident just before we were married."

"So you're the last Farmer?" George sounded . . . skeptical?

Gerty blinked. "Why, I guess I am. I hadn't thought about it quite like that."

Because she suddenly looked so sad, Candy brought up the one subject guaranteed to put fire in Gerty Farmer's eye. "There's Duff."

Duff Farmer was a bluff, portly man with a penchant for Old Milwaukee, the San Francisco 49ers, and his brassy wife, Ethel May. In that order. His loud claims to distant kinship never failed to nettle Gerty straight into a huff.

Angry color infused the older woman's face. "*That man!*" Gerty always called Duff *that man* and Ethel

May *that woman*, lacing two words with more disdain than most people could load into your average tirade.

George lifted an eyebrow. "Duff?"

Tongue in cheek, Candy offered, "Duff is—"

"A no-account piece of trash. One of the black-sheep Farmers," Gerty interjected waspishly. "They claim they're distant relatives. Well, if they are, they're very distant." Obviously not distant enough for Gerty.

Candy rubbed her nose to cover a grin. "Now, Gerty, Duff isn't so bad. He's—"

"A shiftless good-for-nothing who never did an honest day's work in his life! He and *that woman* lived off the government for years."

"Then I guess it's lucky for taxpayers everywhere that Duff came into that money a couple years ago."

George's gaze sharpened. "Money?"

"Yes," muttered Gerty, "but the good Lord only knows where it came from. *That man* is a natural-born shady operator. I don't trust him."

Candy started to object then thought better of it. Duff definitely had a touch of snake-oil salesman. "He might be an operator, but I don't think he'd do anything illegal."

Gerty sniffed but forbore comment.

Running a finger through the condensation on his glass, George asked, "Does he live around here?"

"To my everlasting sorrow." Gerty took a wrathful bite of pizza and chewed vigorously.

"They bought a place over on Horseshoe Bar Road last year." Candy smothered a grin. "It's a real show-case."

Gerty puffed up like an indignant hen. "Showcase?

Plastic animals in the front yard? And that tacky fountain? It most certainly is not a showcase. It's gaudy and ostentatious and—"

"And they're hardly ever there," Candy finished with a meaningful nod toward a rapt Sara. Ruffling Gerty's feathers had been fun until she'd realized the moppet with the mouth was probably storing it all away for future broadcast.

Flashing a guilty glance at her granddaughter, Gerty mumbled, "For which blessing we are truly thankful."

George wiped his fingers on a napkin. "The black-sheep Farmers travel a lot, I take it?"

Candy nodded. "They've been gone a couple of months this time."

"Yes, well, unfortunately, they're coming back next Friday," groused Gerty, and muttered something about bad pennies.

The rest of the evening passed uneventfully, but Candy didn't really relax until she and George were racing away in his Jeep. She leaned her head against the seat, enjoying the way the wind tossed her hair while the scenery rushed by in shadows.

"What a day!" She groaned. "If I never live another like it, it'll be too soon."

"Why do you say that?"

Out of the corner of her eye she saw George's thigh flex as he worked the clutch. Faded jeans hugged his muscular quadriceps. Candy tried very hard not to think about the other body parts they hugged.

It wasn't as easy as it should have been.

Closing her eyes, she stifled a heartfelt groan.

"Candy?"

"Huh?" Her eyes snapped open. Thankful for the darkness that hid her guilty blush, she said, "What?"

"What was so bad about this particular day?"

"Oh. Wagging tongues and prying eyes. You know, George, maybe we should cool it a little. Stay away from each other for a while and give the gossip a chance to die down."

Maybe then her hormones would simmer down so she could think straight. She had an investigation to conduct, and they were getting in the way.

"I don't care about gossip," he growled, turning in to her driveway.

"But—"

"Forget it." He climbed out and circled around to open her door.

Firming up her resolve, Candy nodded her thanks and stepped down. "No, I think we should stop seeing each other for a while."

"Listen, Candy—"

Decision made, she unlocked her door and swung around to say a quick thanks and good night and don't call me, I'll call you. "Thanks for the pizza and everything. Maybe we can do it again sometime. I'll—" *See you around* got blocked by George's mouth.

It was just a brush of lips with a hint of tongue. It shouldn't have been kiss enough to make her stupid. But there she stood, staring up at him, thinking idiotic things like, *Now what was I saying and why should I care?*

A long-overdue breath later she remembered. "Right. Well, I'll—" She might have gotten it out that time if she hadn't made the incredibly dumb mistake of meeting his gaze.

The glint in his eye could best be described as predatory. Hungry. Hot, hot, hot. Candy swallowed and started to close the door. "I'll—I'll—" What?

"Ask me in."

Uh-uh. Nope. No way. Asking him in would be a bad idea. She tried to tell him so, but her lips wouldn't move, and the shake of her head was too slight to be convincing.

He spread his wide palm on the door and pushed inward. Leaned down to brush another kiss across her mouth. "Ask me in, Candy."

He didn't wait for an answer but backed her into the house. Lost in steamy gray eyes, Candy retreated as he closed the door and came toward her. Sometime between the second she came up against the wall and the moment he skimmed his fingers up her neck, the word *stop* disappeared from her vocabulary.

He cradled her face and tilted it up, and she knew he didn't intend to limit himself to a kiss. *Run for your life*, still part of her vocabulary, drifted through the haze in her head. Then his mouth crashed down on hers and blew her whole dictionary straight to hell.

SIX

He'd acted the perfect gentleman, more or less, and what thanks did he get? She tried to give him the brush.

Okay, lady, no more Mr. Nice Geek.

Price angled his head and kissed Candy until her knees buckled and her hands fisted in his shirt. He pulled back to nip her lips, stroke his thumbs across her cheekbones, and growl, "Hang on tight, baby," a heartbeat before he dragged her right back under.

Her mouth was soft, honey with a touch of spice, and he couldn't get enough of it. The taste sent blood thundering through his veins, and all of a sudden he was afraid he'd never get enough of it. Of her, dammit.

His move must have caught her by surprise, because she was pliant. To hell with that, he thought, and drove his tongue deeper. He didn't want her pliant. He wanted her wild. For him.

He drew both hands down her throat over her collarbone to her breasts and traced light circles with his thumbs. Her nipples peaked, her arms shot around his waist, she arched against him, and groaned into his mouth.

He skimmed his hands down her sides and hips, leaning into her to fuse their bodies from chest to groin. She felt so damned good, his lungs locked. Tearing his mouth away, he dropped his head against the wall. "Oh, Candy."

She gasped and wriggled and almost sent him over the edge. "We shouldn't—" He kissed her again, and she moaned. "Damn you, George."

"Later."

"Yeah, later." Her arms tightened and her lips cruised his jaw toward his mouth. She kissed him, and it was one hell of a kiss. The top of his head threatened immediate lift-off.

A couple degrees shy of spontaneous combustion, he lifted his head, closed his eyes, and swallowed. "Let's go someplace more comfortable." More comfortable meaning horizontal. He straightened and swung toward the living room.

Her showgirl legs twined around his waist, her arms around his neck. "This probably isn't a good idea, you know." She bit his earlobe, and he stumbled.

"No, no. This is a great idea." He carried her to the sofa, ready to explode because the friction was killing him. He sat, holding her on his lap while he whipped off his glasses and laid them on the coffee table. "This is probably the greatest idea ever."

"I don't—"

"Trust me." He slid one hand up her back into her hair and tugged, baring her throat to a string of hungry kisses. He lapped at the pulse throbbing in her neck, and she shivered. "See?"

Her hands dropped to his shoulders, and her fingers clenched as she wailed softly, "How do you *do* this to me?"

"Well, like this." He bent her backward and closed his mouth over her breast.

"Oh, God."

He suckled one breast then the other. When he finally lifted his head, Candy was breathing in ragged gasps. Her white blouse clung to her breasts in transparent patches. He reached up to paint an index finger over the lace edge of her bra. "Let's get you out of these."

Peeling her out of her blouse and bra wasn't easy, because her hands kept getting in his way. Since she happened to be ripping the buttons off his blue chambray shirt at the time, he didn't complain.

He stared at her breasts—pert, plump, and crowned with tight pink buds—and his mouth went dry. "Oh, sweetheart, you're—"

"Gorgeous," she purred, and swept her hands over his shoulders, pecs, and belly. Muscles jumped and nerves twitched in her wake. "Absolutely gorgeous." Her hands coasted back up, her arms slid around his neck, and she pressed close. "Mmm. You feel good."

No kidding. If he felt any better he'd explode. So of course he smoothed his hands up her silky back and flattened her against him. She turned her head. His lips grazed her cheek and found her mouth.

With a lithe twist he lay back on the sofa, pulling her down on top of him, shifting until her legs fell on either side of his. With her chest against his, he felt their two hearts rapping to the same jackhammer beat. One hand stroked down her back to mold her buttocks and press while he moved against her.

She whimpered and strained against him, teetering on that fine, sharp edge between control and insanity. The way she responded to his slightest touch set him on fire. His own control unraveled to its last frayed thread. Grimly determined to drive her to the peak, he grabbed that thread and hung on as he quickly unsnapped and unzipped her jeans and slid his hand inside.

His fingers slid down between her legs. Her mouth broke away from his, and she buried her face in his neck. He stroked and caressed, kissing her deeply, willing her to let go for him, and finally she did. He felt the climax roll through her and almost went out of his mind.

"Holy cow," she murmured, and looked dazed, sated, and shocked, all at the same time.

He would have laughed, but figured he'd hurt himself. Instead he shifted her so she lay beside him, and reached for the waistband on her jeans.

In just a few seconds, he promised himself, desperately struggling to peel away the last barriers between them, *I'll be inside of her*. Denim and lace inched down her hips.

God, he wanted her. He'd never felt this way before. Never needed a woman this badly. And he couldn't think of a single reason he shouldn't give in to what he needed right now.

Of course, that was before the dead mouse plopped onto his chest.

Charlie Cheddar reached into his pocket. The crowd squealed adoringly. "We're almost exac'ly five, Charlie." With a benign smile and a regal nod of his head, Charlie tossed mice to his subjects.

And across the room stood Candy. Somehow he knew nobody else could see her—she was there for him alone. Her milky breasts were dappled with color from the flashing lights, her nipples tight buds of arousal. She held out her arms. "I want you." Her lips formed the words he couldn't hear. "Come to me."

He tried. But Geb was there, cursing women and pulling him back into the shadows, reminding him that he had lies to tell and buys to make.

Candy held out an imploring hand. "I need you."

He needed her too. Ferociously. With superhuman effort, Price broke away from Geb and started across the room. Suddenly he was wading through a waist-high sea of rodents.

"Please, George, please."

He could hear her now. He wanted to tell her he was coming, that George wasn't his name. He wanted her to say his real name. He had to know she wanted the man behind the mask. He ached to tell her the truth, but old falsehoods weighed leaden on his tongue.

Still tossing mice, Charlie Cheddar stepped in front of him and said, "Go to her."

Couldn't they see he was trying? He struggled on, straining toward something he didn't understand, something real and good and lasting. He craved it, was desperate to grab and hold it. But the sea of mice was rising, threatening to drown him, and he was so tired. . . .

Too many mice. There were too many mice. . . .

"Too many—" Price lurched up in bed and nearly strangled himself with sheets. He threw a wild look around the room, half expecting to find tiny corpses piled in drifts against the wall, feeling ridiculously relieved because the only body in the room was his.

"Damn." He tugged the bed sheet from around his neck and slid up against the headboard.

The dream would be funny, except the inexplicable feeling that he'd lost something precious lingered. He shook his head in disgust and washed a shaky hand over his sweaty face. Nuts.

The mice. His sense of humor kicked in, inspiring a weary chuckle. No doubt about it, there were too many mice in his life these days.

Having a cat drop a soggy trophy on your bare chest had to be a first. It definitely beat cold showers when it came to dousing a man's enthusiasm. Given Candy's fiery blush and desperate scramble for her discarded shirt, he'd had no choice but to face the glum fact that they weren't going to finish what they'd started. So he'd praised his small buddy, picked up his shirt, and gone home.

As sure as his alias was George Price, Candy would pull in like a box turtle after tonight. Well, she could pull in until the Cubs took the Series in four straight, it wouldn't do her any good.

He had an itch only she could scratch, a staggering admission for a man who'd always viewed female bodies as more or less interchangeable. But this one woman was the only woman who would do.

Dammit.

He raked his fingers through his hair and tossed an annoyed glance at the clock. Bilious green, three A.M. glowered back at him. Too much night left for a man who wouldn't sleep anytime soon. He smiled sardonically and reached for the phone. Misery was about to wake up some company.

"Company" took six rings to rouse and answered with a grunt.

"Morning, Geb."

"Morn—" A string of curses punctuated by clatter, followed by fumbling and more swearing. "Dropped the damned phone. You still there?"

"Yep." Leisurely, Price crossed his ankles. "I didn't get you up, did I?"

"Yeah, but that's all—" Geb's voice sharpened. "What's wrong?"

"Nothing's wrong."

"Nothing's wrong." Pause. Then, progressing from a low growl to a near roar: "You called me at three in the friggin' mornin' just to tell me nothing's wrong?"

Price's lips twitched. "You never heard about reach out and touch someone?"

"Man, I am gonna reach out and touch you upside your head."

"Will you reconsider if I tell you I got a lead on Farmer?"

Geb swore again. Price could almost see him run long, tapered fingers over his gleaming crown. "I might. What you got?"

"Confirmation. Duff Farmer was a well-known welfare mooch and all-around lazy bum right up until the day he breezed into a mysterious windfall some two years ago."

"Timing's right. Big windfall?"

"Enough cold hard cash to cough up two hundred thou for the Taj Mahal of bad taste he built here in town, not to mention sufficient residual bread to finance a couple cars and one or two prolonged world tours."

"Damn. You two connected yet?"

"Haven't had a chance. He and his old lady aren't back from their latest jaunt."

"Time's runnin' out. Nelson's getting antsy in Anaheim, and we gotta move on this."

Price rubbed the back of his neck. "I know. Rumor has it he'll be back in town next Friday."

"Too late. You and him got to be tight before things start happenin', or we're gonna lose the buy."

"We are not going to lose the buy."

"No?" Geb snorted. "Suppose you tell me how you're gonna stop it? Farmer ain't gonna deal with some greasy-headed fool he doesn't know from Adam."

"Dammit, the greasy-headed fool was all your idea!" Geb grumbled something about raw material, but Price ignored him. "Farmer might not like, know, or trust me, but he'll deal."

"Now, why would he do that?"

"I'll make him an offer he can't refuse."

Geb hummed with satisfaction. "You've got something on him."

"Not yet, but the house is empty and I have six days to toss it."

"Are we talking about breaking and entering?"

"B and E? Me?" Price tried on his best Beaver Cleaver. "Golly, Geb, that's illegal!"

"Jive turkey," muttered Geb, but chuckled. "Just make sure you don't end up with the local cops chewing your sorry butt."

"The local cops are named Hiram Walters. Fifty-four, balding, with a beer gut. That bohunk couldn't find his own butt with both hands, let alone chew mine."

"Yeah, well, you'll pardon my skepticism, but you're oh for one with bohunks so far."

"What's that supposed to mean?"

"The nosy gym teacher."

"She's no bohunk." The words popped out without thought. Thought leaped close behind and had Price silently cursing his big mouth.

"Is that right?" Geb drawled after a surprised silence. "What is she?"

Trouble. But he managed to keep that behind his teeth. "Wrapped around my little finger."

That he'd never managed to sneak a lie past Jamal Gebhardt was a fact he remembered too late.

"Be damned," Geb breathed. "She got to you, didn't she? Man, this Candy Johnson must be one hell of a lady to tie *you* up in knots."

"You say that like tying me up in knots ranks right up there with walking on water."

"Oh, it does. You, my friend, are what's known as unknottable. Leastwise, you always have been." Price gave that observation a two-word evaluation, and Geb laughed. "That *would* smooth out the kinks."

Price grinned ruefully and shook his head. "Yeah, well, I'm working on it."

"Uh-huh. You *do* have one or two other little issues to work out, pal. Try not to forget that."

Trying hard not to think about what had been a very close call, Candy slipped off her shirt then froze, staring dumbly at her bare breasts. Good Lord, she'd forgotten to put on her bra. "Oh."

Hotly embarrassed, she shook off her paralysis and spun toward the bathtub, flinging aside the curtain, wrenching taps, and muttering. Water shot from the shower head. She straightened, reaching for the snap on her jeans, still trying not to think.

Because if she thought, she'd think about the things George had done to her. And the things he hadn't. Then she'd probably run over to his apartment and attack him for two or three days.

"Stop thinking about it!" she said, and dove for the shower.

"Damned menace." Snatching up a bottle, she dumped shampoo onto her head and scoured resolutely, as if she could wash away the thoughts that still threatened.

Sometime between the drying off and slipping into a nightshirt, fatigue crashed down on her. Her arms and legs turned to rubber, her brain to a thick pool of molasses. The last time she'd felt this woozy she'd been

five and her six-year-old brother, Brian, had just
beaned her with a Louisville Slugger.

But tired or not, when she reached the bed she had
to stop and grin.

Columbo lay sprawled on his back amid the royal-
blue peonies strewn across her bedspread, the image of
indolent feline repletion. A cat chock-full of mouse and
himself.

"You," she said, lightly scratching his bulging belly,
"are a good friend, and you saved me from myself."

Briefly cracking one eye, Columbo sent her a lazy
snatch of purr before drifting back into his stupor. He
didn't so much as twitch a whisker when she scooped
her hands under him and slid him to the other side of
the bed.

Giving in to a giant yawn, she thought she might
sleep for a week. She peeled back the covers and
crawled into bed, her body melting into a boneless
puddle. Her eyelids sank like lead weights.

Her brain was slower to wind down, replaying the
day's most humiliating clips and rehashing the torrid
encounter with George in vivid detail. Detail that had
her tired body tingling in spite of itself.

Nobody, she mused drowsily, had ever made her
feel that way. She hadn't known she *could* feel that way.
Too bad she'd decided not to see George again. Any
man who could make you feel like that was certainly
worth knowing. Heck, a man who could make you feel
like that could be downright addictive.

But she still didn't trust him, and she wasn't ready
to be addicted to one man, especially one who would
put a crimp in her career plans. In a couple years she'd

be ready to make the leap into her new, exciting life, and somehow she just couldn't see George Price trotting the globe in search of danger and intrigue.

She was a breath away from sleep when a new thought prickled at the edge of consciousness. It prickled and nagged and pushed until it finally wormed its way to the front of her brain.

George had been pumping Gerty Farmer for information.

Slowly, unwillingly, Candy's heavy eyelids rose to half-mast. Exhaustion layered her mind like thick cobwebs; she struggled to clear them away and think.

He'd been digging for information. Anesthetized by encroaching sleep, Candy was only mildly irked by the fact that George was better at interrogation than she was.

Her eyes closed, and her thoughts drifted in spite of her best efforts to hold them steady. This newest evidence was important. She ought to think it through and follow it up.

But she'd already decided to steer clear of George Price, so follow-up wasn't going to happen.

One last admission floated lazily through her brain, followed by an ironclad resolution. She was curious again. But for once in her life, she absolutely would *not* give in to curiosity.

SEVEN

4:12 A.M.

Megavolt undercurrents tonight. And that intermittent gleam in his eye—shrewd. Calculating.

Tugging the sheet up under her chin, Candy sniffed sleepily. *George Price shrewd and calculating? Get real.*

"No gleam," she mumbled. "Reflection. Flashing lights and Coke bottles."

George Price calculating. Amused, she drifted back to sleep.

5:29 A.M.

He asked about Duff's money. Twice.

Candy groaned, rolled onto her stomach, and groped for a pillow, dragging it over her head on the groggy premise that what was good for the ostrich was good for inquisitive birdbrains too.

Curiouser and curiouser, nagged relentless suspicion.

Put a sock in it, Alice. Determined, Candy struggled back into the arms of Morpheus.

6:17 A.M.

He was certainly interested in Duff's trip—in all of Duff's trips. Not to mention Duff's cars and Duff's house. Kind of makes you wonder, doesn't it?

"No, no, no." Candy belly-crawled backward until blankets shrouded her from head to toe. "I *don't* wonder," she moaned. "I don't."

7:30 A.M.

She was wide-awake, glowering at the ceiling through eyeballs the texture of two-twenty-gauge sandpaper while her head throbbed dully. She was cranky.

Curiosity was eating her alive. Knowing she was going to give in to it made her even crankier.

Snug against her hip, Columbo woke up with a languid stretch. His eyes opened slowly. Their gazes locked, piercing yellow to bloodshot blue. The cat squawked, flipped to his feet, and shot under the nightstand.

"Smart move." Candy and her attitude flounced out of bed.

She waited for that first, lifesaving cup to trickle through the coffeemaker and stewed about sexual chemistry. Seeing George again was risky. Bones would be jumped the minute they got together. Knowing she might be the first to pounce didn't sweeten her disposition.

But doubts and questions chafed like a rash— sooner or later they'd drive her crazy. George could give her the answers and relief. Then again, if she got within fifty feet of him, her hormones would drive her crazy. He could give her relief for that too.

"Damn menace."

Snatching the carafe from under the dripper, she poured a scant half mug of coffee and knocked it back straight, scalding her tongue. Swearing like a sailor, she clapped a hand over her mouth and lunged for the freezer.

A couple of minutes later caffeine jump-started her flagging brain. Sucking meditatively on an ice cube, Candy thought about damage control. It was going to be tricky.

Proximity and privacy were her enemies. She had to get close enough to pry, but stay out of reach. Unfortunately, George had long arms and a problem keeping them to himself.

Maybe if she met him in a public place . . .

Suddenly she remembered a debauched thumb doing wicked things to her heart rate as it stroked her palm and wrist.

In a public place.

Her shoulders drooped. Candy slid the ice cube out of her mouth and groaned. "Damn!" She tossed the ice remnant into the sink and turned toward the bedroom. Her morning run would untangle the old thought processes. Jogging always—

She skidded to a stop in the doorway. Her eyes widened with glee. "Jogging! Yes!" She punched a fist into the air and sent the cautiously emerging Columbo scuttling back under cover.

Feeling benevolent for having finally hit on a solution, Candy knelt in front of the nightstand. "Come on out, chum," she crooned, reaching in to sweep him into her arms, where she could stroke his head. "I've been a real witch this morning, haven't I?"

Columbo eyed her sullenly. *"Mmmrow."*

Miffed by his ready agreement, she narrowed her eyes. "Oh, yeah. Like *you've* never been in a snit." Columbo lifted his nose and leaped out of her arms. "See?" she said to his tail as he padded haughtily out of the room. "Goofy cat." Dismissing him with a shrug, Candy wheeled toward the dresser.

In no time at all she was dressed for action, her gray shorts bagging to her knees, a tattered blue jersey bagging everywhere else. Seen fore and aft in a full-length mirror, the outfit fit her like a bad tent, sloppy and shapeless. Absolutely sexless. Perfect.

She strode into the living room to pick up the phone and put her latest plan into action. Get the answers she needed without the sex she didn't—well, without the sex, anyway.

George was potent, but he couldn't seduce on the run.

She hoped.

"Run?" Price cleared the sleep out of his throat. Two measly hours' worth didn't take much of a gargle. "You want me to *run* with you?"

"Actually, it would be more of a jog."

Scrubbing a hand over his bristled jaw, he queried his body. If he really pushed it, he might work up a slow shuffle. "Jog?"

"Uh-huh. You know, that thing where you go faster than a walk but slower than a dash?"

"Cute, Johnson." She sounded so damned chipper. He tried not to hold it against her.

"George?"

"Yeah." Fumbling for the clock, he held it up and squinted bleary eyes. Eight A.M. *Now?*

"Sure. Morning's the best time for a pleasant jog."

Pleasant jog was an oxymoron. Running for the hell of it was all sweat and strain and sheer boredom. He'd take the battling blood lust of down-and-dirty handball or cutthroat one-on-one any day. But even as *forget it* hovered on his tongue, he hesitated.

Last night she'd been in full retreat, this morning she was making a move. What was wrong with this scenario? He hedged, buying time to figure it out. "I'm not much of a runner."

"You're not?" Was that disappointment? "Oh. That's too bad." Definitely disappointment. "I guess I'll see you around sometime, then." Followed by yet another attempted kiss-off.

So it was jog or good-bye, Charlie. She'd see him again on her terms. Well, only a fool slammed the door in opportunity's face because he didn't like the rap of her knuckles. "I said I'm not much of a runner, I didn't say I never run."

"So you'll go?" They were back to chipper.

He sighed. "Yeah, I'll go." Not quickly or well, but he'd go. "Give me a few minutes to get dressed, and I'll be over."

"*No!* Er . . . I mean, I'm ready to go out the door. How 'bout I pick you up?"

Her terms all the way, then, he thought, and his lips curved slowly. "Fine. Twenty minutes?"

"Right. See you then."

Since when, he wondered as he dragged his weary bones toward the bathroom, had a couple sleepless nights slowed him down? No, more than a couple, he realized abruptly. Between scam-related frustration and sexual frustration, he'd been sleepless or near sleepless for weeks.

Insomnia was a habit he had to break. Immediately. Things would hit the fan any day now; either he got his head one hundred percent screwed on, or he caught the fallout. It was time to shape up.

When he opened the door to Candy's knock, he was forced to face the pitiful shape he was in.

Last night, half-naked and rosy with passion, she'd been the sexiest woman he'd ever seen. This morning she was an unqualified mess. Her eyes were a puffy red, white, and blue; her hair closely resembled Albert Einstein's. She wore no makeup, she was dressed like a Goodwill reject, and she was *still* the sexiest woman he'd ever seen.

It didn't get more pitiful than that.

"Hi." Her eyes zeroed in on his bare chest, dropped to his cutoffs, and widened, scampered down his legs, then zoomed back to his face—all in a little over a second. "So." Her voice had gone husky. "Are you all warmed up?"

They were *both* all warmed up, if her throat and his groin were anything to go by. All of a sudden running for the hell of it made perfect sense, and the sooner the better. He hooked a blue-and-white Dodgers T-shirt over his head. "Yeah, let's go."

The sun beat down on them, slicing off the shadow of George's apartment building and shrinking his pupils to pinpoints as his muscles lumbered into action. His first pounding strides jounced loose a stream of silent curses. For five eternal minutes he was sure he was dying.

But then death would have been a blessing.

"Isn't this great?" chirped Candy. Damned if she didn't sound like she meant it too.

Price grunted and swerved to avoid a head-on collision with a redheaded hit-and-run artist doing Mach five on a tricycle. "Yeah, great."

Above the deafening rasp of his own breathing he thought he heard her chuckle. "Atta boy, Flash."

"Smart aleck." Too bad he liked that in a woman.

By the time they rounded the corner, he'd smoothed out his Quasimodo gallop. Muscles loosened and warmed, his lungs finally started drawing breaths bigger than a teaspoon.

Candy flashed him a grin. "Now you're cooking with gas. Another quart of endorphins and you'll sprint right into a runner's high."

He grunted. "Like hell."

She chuckled again and pointed down the block. "Let's cut through the park."

"The park." His gaze swung left. Trees. Shade. Grass cushion. "Right."

Blue sky gave way to green canopy. Sifted through leaves and branches, the blazing sun scattered pale splotches across the dirt path under their feet.

He glanced sideways, planning to adjust his stride to match Candy's. Unfortunately, the sight of trim calves in motion turned what should have been a brief, impersonal check into a hungry leer with all too predictable results.

Eyes front, bozo. Look at the nice park.

"Quite a crowd," he mused.

"Surprised?"

"Nope. I've been in town long enough to catch on to the Farmer Brown schedule. Go to bed with the chickens, get up with the chickens."

"And if it's Saturday, you go to the park."

"Straight out of *Our Town*," he decided with a nod toward two teenagers. The pair strolled hand in hand, wrapped up in each other and oblivious to everything else. "Or Norman Rockwell," he added as he watched a pack of boys dart, duck, and jockey on a basketball court.

He and Candy followed the path's meandering course around a mini-metropolis of playground equipment. Kids swarmed up the jungle gym and zipped down the slide, laughing and shouting while their parents watched and traded gossip on shady benches.

Suddenly memories sliced through him, sickle-sharp, of a life he'd left without one look back. Until now. Past and present clashed as he came face-to-face with things he'd never faced before.

Desperate for a little perspective, he tried a wisecrack. "Typical small-town Saturday morning. Hard to believe I missed out on all this excitement growing up."

But his attempt at dry humor sounded embarrassingly like sour grapes.

Candy shot him an inquisitive glance as they cantered from shady park to sunny sidewalk. "You grew up in the city?"

"Lady, I grew up in hell's backyard." It bypassed his brain and babbled straight out of his mouth. He blinked, wondering if he'd jogged completely out of his mind.

Telling the truth wasn't smart. But all of a sudden he realized he *wanted* to tell . . . well, some of it. What he didn't know was why.

It scared the crap out of him.

They trotted past Larson's. Candy waved to the old woman pyramiding dog-food cans in the display window, and Edwina Bimson returned an encouraging thumbs-up that had his lips twitching while his gut churned.

Candy pointedly cleared her throat. "So where *is* hell's backyard, geographically speaking?"

It wasn't too late to lie. He didn't. "South-central L.A."

"Does your family still live there?"

"My mother lived in the same three-room walk-up until the day she died. Five years after I left, I went back with the idea of buying her a house in a better neighborhood. She wasn't interested."

"She liked the old neighborhood?"

He cursed the embarrassing impulse to talk even as he continued to give in to it. Voice carefully neutral, he said, "She turned my offer down cold. Joan was good at cold, not so good at motherhood. I was a living reminder of the one time she sobered up enough to have sex and get pregnant. She could barely stand to look at me, much less take anything from me."

Silence. Then: "What about your father?"

"Beats me. I never laid eyes on the man."

"You—" She broke off.

"It happens."

"Yeah. I guess. So what did you do for fun in hell's backyard?"

"Same as kids everywhere, I guess. Hung out, played ball. There were four of us," he remembered, and surprised himself by smiling after all. "A beat-up basketball and a vacant lot between two buildings. We'd imagine hoops perched up on the dirty brick and elbow the hell out of each other trying to get in a shot."

"And then you grew up."

"Not quite. First I dropped out of school and into trouble. Lucked out with probation. *Then* I grew up. Went after my GED, enlisted, and let Uncle Sam take me away from it all." He tossed off a shrug and lengthened his stride, determined to outstrip the pity that was sure to follow.

Candy hung back for a minute before catching up with him—effortlessly, dammit. "You left the army, went to college, got your teaching degree, and lived happily ever after."

"Close enough." He slid her a glance. "What? No tongue clucking and head pats?"

"I'm not the type."

"No, you're not, are you?" His shoulder muscles uncoiled in relief. He jogged on silently, determined to get a grip on his loose lips before he went down like the *Titanic*.

"Well, George, you know what they say."

He swiped at the sweat beading his forehead. "No. What do they say?"

"You've come a long way, baby."

"I don't know about that," he muttered. He was pathetically grateful when Candy hung another left to head back toward his place.

"Just a few more blocks." She sounded encouraging.

"Right. No problem." He could keep his mouth shut for a few more blocks. Probably. Figuring his mouth couldn't run off half-cocked if he kept it full of questions, he asked, "What about you?"

"What about me what?"

"Have you come a long way?"

"George, I haven't come at all," she said, and broke out in a neck-to-hairline blush. "I didn't mean—" Her mouth snapped shut. He heard her draw a deep breath. "What I meant to say," she continued deliberately, "was that I'm stuck following family tradition. Sort of. For now."

"You come from a long line of teachers?"

"That's where the sort of comes in."

"You *sort of* come from a long line of teachers?"

"I come from a long line of athletes. Teaching phys ed was their idea of a compromise."

"Oh." He paused and shook his head. "I don't get it. Compromise for what?"

"The thrill of victory, gold medals, and world records."

"We're talking really good athletes here, right?"

"Oh, they're good." She sounded glum. "My brother Brian—"

The bell rang, loud and clear. "Brian Johnson." He turned his head to gape and almost tripped on a crack in the sidewalk. "Your brother is Brian Johnson? Good grief! He just set a new record in the triathlon!"

Candy's smile was both proud and pained. "Yeah. Eric was mad enough to gnaw the points off his ski poles. He wanted to set the first record."

"Eric Johnson, downhill racer. Favored in the winter games." On the heels of that realization, a half-remembered headline. "Ten, maybe fifteen years ago at Wimbledon, Jack and Gail Johnson. Everybody thought they were too old to win the mixed doubles."

She nodded. "Mom and Dad still play, but that was their last tournament. Just your typical Johnson blaze of glory."

"Damn, woman! That's not a family, that's a regular *Who's Who in Sports*! No wonder you run like a frigging gazelle! Hell, you've got jock genes coming out your ears. Coordination up the wazoo. Why aren't you out whipping butt and winning medals?"

She looked disgruntled. "I tried."

"And?"

"The butt that got whipped was usually mine."

"In what sport?"

"Track and field."

"What else?" He slanted her a skeptical look. "You know, we've been clipping along for at least thirty minutes, and only one of us is breathing hard. I'm pretty sure you could run from here to Poughkeepsie."

"So?"

"So you're telling me you were a track-and-field washout?" He snorted. "Get serious."

"Already there."

"You lost?"

"Repeatedly."

"Yeah?" She nodded, and he gestured helplessly. "But . . . how?"

"Let's just say I'm competitively challenged."

"Competitively challenged?"

Through gritted teeth: "I'm a wimp."

"Huh?"

"A wimp!" she bellowed. "I'm the original nice guy and I always finish last! Got it?"

At that volume he'd have to be stone deaf not to. He nodded. "A wimp. Got it."

He tried to choke off the laughter but spotted two slack-jawed girls gawking across a white picket fence. They nodded, too, and he lost it.

"Now look what you made me do." Candy's face glowed scarlet. "Dammit, George, those two are students of mine," she snapped, and he roared. "Stop that!"

Because laughing while jogging threatened to asphyxiate him, he tried to oblige her. But it took him a half block, gasping and weaving, to regain control.

"Fat-headed hyena." She slowed to a walk as they neared his building.

Price knuckled tears of mirth out of his eyes. "Hey, don't blame me. You're the one who delivered the personal news flash at the top of her lungs. I could have hurt myself, you know."

"It's not too late," she mused thoughtfully. "I could help."

Since he wasn't sure she didn't mean it, he quickly changed the subject. "You said for now."

She stopped, scooped damp hair off her forehead, and scowled. "What?"

"You said you were stuck following family tradition, sort of, for now."

"Yeah, so?"

"Simmer down, babe. It occurs to me that you've mentioned a career change more than once. You're planning something. Am I right?"

"Maybe."

"Like pulling teeth," he muttered. "You have a particular career in mind?"

"Yes."

He waited. She let him. He tossed up his hands. "Well?"

She hesitated, eyeing him suspiciously. "If you laugh again, so help me, I'll—"

"I won't laugh." He had a strong hunch that she'd deck him if he did. "I swear."

"A cop."

He felt his jaw drop. "*What?*"

"I think I'd like to be a cop."

"You'd like to be a cop." The irony struck like a fist. Oh yeah, he wanted to laugh. Only she'd never understand that he wouldn't be laughing at her, but at fate and himself.

"Or a private investigator."

"Hmm." Actually, it shouldn't come as a surprise. Her bookshelves packed enough detective stories to bury the entire L.A.P.D. She was snoopy and dogged, with the instincts of Mike Hammer and the moxie of Auntie Mame. In short, she was a natural.

"So what do you think?"

Her expression was a cross between a plea and a dare. "Uh . . . it's great. I think it's great."

"You do?"

"Sure. If that's what you want."

"It is." She looked nonplussed. He knew the feeling. "Most people," she started carefully while watching him like a hawk, "would think my aspirations to cophood were a joke."

"Cops," he said, "are no joke."

"No." Her stare was drawn out and disconcerted. So he'd put her at a loss. In his book, that made them even. "Well, thanks."

"For?"

"Taking me seriously."

Secrets scraped at his conscience. Uncomfortable with the guilt, he shrugged.

Peering at him from under furrowed brows, Candy backed up slowly. "Well. I . . . uh . . . guess I should be going. I've got . . . things. I've got things to do."

"Uh-huh. Me too." Like stop this emotional roller coaster and get the hell off. *No more morning jogs with hot blondes for you, pal—hazardous to your mental health.*

"I'll see you later, then."

"Sure, later."

Chocolate wasn't working.

The most powerful mood-altering drug known to woman had yet to dent Candy's bizarre funk. She took another bite, let the square melt on her tongue, and waited for the buzz.

Nothing.

It was unnatural.

Swearing softly, she tossed the chocolate bar onto the table and reached for the phone. Jen Maddox was the most sensible person in the world. Who better to explain why nothing made sense anymore?

"Maddox residence." It sounded like a challenge. Mrs. Crampton, Jen and Brent's housekeeper, wasn't just built like a tank, she had the personality of one.

Candy grinned in spite of her mood. "Hi, Althea."

"Candy? That you, girl?"

"Uh-huh. How are you?"

"Never mind the chitchat. You find yourself a decent man yet?"

George leaped immediately to mind, and nerves jittered. "I haven't been looking for a decent man."

"Better get to it. You're not getting any younger."

"Thanks for the reminder." Amused at both of them now, Candy hurried to cut off the incipient lecture. "Is Jen there? Can I talk to her?"

"She's here. Hold on while I go peel those two apart."

Candy pictured petite, brunette Jen in a clinch with her big, blond husband, and stiffened. "Peel them apart? Wait, Althea! Don't—"

"Didn't I tell you to hold on?"

The tone had Candy swallowing the rest of her protest. "Yes, ma'am."

A couple of minutes later Jen came on the line. "Candy?"

"Hi, Jen. Hope I didn't call at a . . . um . . . a bad time. How are you?"

"Your timing is fine, and I'm wonderful. Crazy in love with my terrific husband. How about you?"

"Oh, I'm all—actually, I'm a mess."

"What's the problem?" Candy quickly summed up her initial suspicions about George. "And based on flimsy evidence like that, you decided he was an impostor?" Jen squawked in disbelief. "For goodness' sake, Candy—"

"The man infuriated me. So a few weeks ago I decided to check up on him. Expose him, you know? No big deal, right? Except the works have been gummed up ever since."

"You're in some kind of trouble, aren't you?"

"I'll say." Candy swallowed. "Jen . . . I've mellowed."

"I see." Pause. "No, I don't."

"Toward George. He doesn't infuriate me anymore, he only exasperates me. And I . . . well . . . care about him."

Longer pause. Then: "Care?"

Candy snorted. "Right. Who am I trying to kid? I'm obsessed. George Price, God's little joke on the fashion industry, makes my mouth water. He really is such a menace," she finished gloomily.

"Look, I don't see the problem here—"

"I'm getting to the problem here. My attitude

toward George has done a complete one-eighty. And as if that weren't idiotic enough, now I've come down with this new strain of insanity."

"You're losing me."

"He's on the level, Jen."

"That's it, I'm lost."

"Pay attention. George is on the level. I have to hand it to him; once he decided to be forthcoming, he did it with style. You wouldn't want to hear about what passed for his childhood. Of course he tried to leech all the emotion out of the story. Hell," she grumbled, "he might as well tattoo 'Don't pity me' across his forehead. Fine. I can take a hint."

"And what he doesn't know won't irritate and embarrass him?"

"Exactly. But I'm not moping around, stuffing my face with Hershey's best because George had a rotten boyhood. Of course, if I could get my hands on those so-called parents of his—" Candy broke off for a calming breath. "George got over it, and so will I. At least now I understand his attitude. The bad news is," she concluded glumly, "that I believe he's exactly who he says he is."

Jen cleared her throat. "And . . . this is a problem?"

"Well, sure."

"That's crazy. Finding out George is trustworthy is a good thing."

"Uh-huh."

"The logical reaction would be relief."

"Right." Good old Jen. Always sensible. "He understands me, you know." The way her family never had. "He encourages my plans. Since the man is the magnet to my pig iron, I should be turning handsprings."

"See there?"

"I'm miserable."

"Oh, for—why?"

"Case closed, Jen. I've lost my excuse to hang around him. That's depressing enough, but I suddenly realized that the 'case' has been nothing *but* an excuse for weeks now. What am I going to do?" she wailed in near despair.

"I'm beginning to get the picture. You don't just care about this man, you *care* about him. And now that your suspicions have disappeared, you don't have any reason to keep him at arm's length."

"Yeah. He's no longer forbidden fruit. The menace."

"So why don't you grab him?"

"Because this grab-George urge is too powerful. It worries me. I can't come up with an explanation for it. There's lust, of course," she mused, "and—" Her eyes widened. "*Oh, my God!*"

"Love," Jen guessed, with what sounded like a great deal of satisfaction. "It's the real thing this time, isn't it? I'm so glad. If you hadn't triple-dog-dared me to write that letter to *Celebrity* magazine, Brent wouldn't have seen it and come back to Donnerton, and we would never have gotten together. I can never thank you enough for that, Candy. And now you'll be as happy as I am. This is wonderful! Wait until I tell Brent and Althea."

Heart drumming, Candy cradled her forehead in

one hand. "Hold it a minute. Just hold it." She drew a shaky breath, trying to marshal all the arguments that would prove that Jen was absolutely wrong.

"Well?"

"George is no Brent Maddox. He's not classy and sweet-tempered and good-looking. He's surly and pig-headed and a nerd and . . . Oh, God. I *can't* love him," she insisted desperately. "Maybe it's just a temporary delusion."

Jen's knowing chuckle brought on a new wave of panic. "Sure. And if it's not?"

Candy closed her eyes on a heartfelt groan. "In that case, I'm going to need a lot more chocolate."

EIGHT

Jim Morrison wanted his fire lit. Candy thought lighting your man's fire was a wonderful idea. As a matter of fact, she looked forward to her own personal conflagration.

Humming along with The Doors, she checked her hip gyration while she stroked on mascara. She straightened and tilted her head, studying the results. Her smile blossomed, satisfied and slightly predatory. Batting her lashes, she purred to her reflection, "Why, Grandma, what big eyes you have."

All the better to ogle him with, my dear.

Morrison sang that he had no time to wallow in the mire, and Candy nodded briskly. "You got that right, Jimmy. It's been three days. I've had it up to here with mire-wallowing."

A school-night seduction might not be ideal, but there was no way she could hold off until this weekend. George would have to cope.

She danced into the bedroom grinning mid-pirouette at the innocent-looking box on her dresser. The swatches of lace and satin she'd ordered from Victoria's Secret on a long-ago whim weren't remotely innocent.

George didn't stand a chance.

You're in too deep and moving way too fast. This is a bad idea, whispered a voice in her head.

"It is not," Candy snapped. Common sense was murder on a woman's fantasies. She snatched up the Victoria's Secret box and marched over to sit on the bed.

It is too. Will you just listen?

"I've been listening all day. Anybody ever tell you you're a real nag?"

The little pest hadn't shut up since Candy decided to get George into bed and take out all her pent-up frustration on him. Candy refused to believe it was love.

The nuisance in her brain snorted.

"What do you know?"

There was something about wispy black underwear that brought out the vamp in a woman, she thought as she smoothed a stocking up her leg and hooked it to the garter belt. She slid her feet into a pair of spiked heels and strolled over to the mirror.

Riveted by her reflection, Candy stared. Her breasts looked impossibly full and creamy, lifted and framed in low-cut black. Somehow she'd grown a mile of leg below her French-cut panties. Dazed by the difference a bare fistful of material made in an ordinary body, she swallowed heavily.

While Morrison wailed hoarsely she decided that lighting George's fire shouldn't be a problem. Unless she missed her guess, this outfit made for one heck of a blowtorch. Too bad she had to cover it up with a dress.

Of course it wasn't much of a dress.

It might have been nerves—or the pressure brought to bear by her red spandex minidress—but by the time she climbed into her car, her heart hovered in her throat.

Second thoughts? offered her hopeful alter ego.

"Not a chance." Hands trembling with a combination of tension and anticipation, Candy switched on the ignition. "I know exactly what I'm doing."

All she needed was the confidence to see it through. So she punched a cassette into the tape player and sang "Long, Cool Woman in a Black Dress" all the way to George's place.

She tucked her Honda into a parallel-parking space in front of the building and tried to reassure the worrywart in her head. Yes, she was doing the right thing. No, she wouldn't get her heart broken. Only people in love got their hearts broken. Ignoring caution's dismayed groan, she drew a deep breath for courage and stepped out.

She didn't notice that George's apartment was dark until she'd already knocked on the door.

It took three rounds of knocks and a chorus of outraged banging to convince her he wasn't home.

"I don't believe this!" Jamming her hands at her hips, Candy pivoted slowly, glaring at the street as if an explanation would drive by any second. "I *do not* believe this!"

She'd bought a new dress and sexy underwear. Squashed a bad case of nerves—and yes, dammit, second thoughts—to drive over and offer herself up on a silver platter. And the overgrown jackass had the sheer, unmitigated gall to be someplace else.

"I could just scream."

She settled for a frustrated growl and stalked back to her car, heels spiking angrily at the sidewalk. "The big dope. When I get my hands on him . . ." Her fingers flexed longingly at her sides.

She jerked open the door. Yanking off her shoes, she pitched them into the car and herself in after them. The engine roared to life as she shoved the Stones into the tape deck and cranked up the volume.

Jagger screamed out, a man short on satisfaction.

"That makes two of us." Candy hit the gas and glared into her rearview mirror. "Dammit, George, where are you?"

He was in Hog Heaven.

Well, right outside the door anyway.

Eighty-six miles south of Donnerton on Interstate 5, Hog Heaven squatted alone on the cusp of a night-shrouded exit ramp, looking more bunker than bar. Harleys canted rank-and-file in the badly lit parking lot, proof that the hot red name glowing over the door owed more to chrome and horsepower than a state of bliss. Favored by bikers and hell-raisers, Heaven was a place where angels feared to tread.

But then angels didn't carry .45 semiautomatics.

Déjà vu was stepping into a smoke-filled room to face a bunch of animals who'd just as soon slit your throat as look at you. The whole scene had Price waxing nostalgic. He'd done some of his best work in joints like this. Which only went to show, he admitted with a tired internal sigh, that his work environment stank.

He paused inside the door. Conversation died and heads swiveled his way. The jukebox pumped raunchy guitar music into thickening silence as malice crackled to life, charging the air like lightning before a strike. Price's stance—head up, legs braced apart, hands loose at his sides—was a blatant challenge.

Take a good look, you bastards.

They did.

Men saw a king-sized son of a bitch nobody with a single working brain cell would hassle. The steely glint in those gray eyes was easy reading: *Ready and more than able to dismantle the first fool who gets in my face.*

There were no fools in Heaven that night.

From the female perspective, there was a lifetime supply of raw male stacked in those leather boots. The black hair brushing the collar of his leather bomber jacket looked thick, wavy, and—like the man himself— not quite tame.

In under sixty seconds the pack classified Price an equal as opposed to fresh meat, and the tide of feral malevolence ebbed. Talk resumed as he sauntered toward the back-corner booth where he'd spotted Gebhardt.

Geb's deep-chocolate eyes danced with amusement as Price slid his long frame onto the cracked vinyl seat. *"All over* junkyard dog."

"What?"

"You got the boys real spooked, man. You even had me scared for a minute there."

"Is that so?"

"Big time. Sure wish I could style like that. Us little guys gotta sweat if we want to come down heavy."

Price eyed his friend. Long and lean and deadly. "You're not little, and the only time I ever saw you sweat was the day your mom came home early from choir practice and caught us drooling over the November Playmate's thirty-eight D's."

Geb winced. "Don't remind me. My whole life flashed in front of my eyes when Mama came after us with that strap."

"Your whole life? We were only ten."

"It was kind of a puny flash. You know, I *still* sweat when she—"

"What'll ya have?" They turned to find the "cocktail waitress" limned in the glow of the jukebox.

She wore boots and jeans and a T-shirt somebody had gnawed sleeveless. Between the explosion of hair, the nose ring, and the python tattoo coiling her arm from wrist to shoulder, the woman was a work of art. *Abstract Expressionist's Nightmare.*

"I haven't got all night," she reminded them.

"Bring us a couple beers." Price eyed the grimy table. "Bottles not glasses."

She snorted loudly. "Good thinkin'."

"Now that," murmured Geb as she stalked off, "is scary."

"Yeah." His gaze swung around to narrow on Geb's face. "You bring the stuff?"

"Uh-huh." Geb reached into his hooded sweatshirt and pulled out a small camera and a rolled-up leather pouch. "But I don't like it. Boss wouldn't either."

"But the boss won't know, will he?"

"Save the you're-a-dead-man stare for the tourists. Any goods the boss gets on you won't come from me or Traynor." He set both the case and camera on the table. " 'Course the cat will jump clean out the bag when you get pinched for B and E."

Price unfurled the pouch to reveal a set of lock picks. "You worry too much. I've told you before, we're not exactly dealing with real cops here. Compared to Donnerton's finest, Barney Fife is Sherlock Holmes. I won't get pinched."

"Make damned sure you don't. There's enough high-grade Colombian on that acreage to keep every pothead in L.A. flyin' for a month. Word on the street says it goes to the highest bidder, but if you get busted for tossing Farmer's crib, we won't be at the auction. Things go down that way, you can kiss your butt good-bye, because there won't be nothin' left but the dimple when the boss gets through with you."

Satisfied with the picks, Price closed up the pouch and tucked it into his inside jacket pocket. He picked up the camera. "Like I said, you worry too much." He peered through the viewfinder. "Built-in flash?"

"Yeah, yeah." Geb ran a hand over his head. "You sure there's no other way? I got a bad feeling about this."

"Don't be such a wimp. There is no other way. The nights are already cold; we'll have frost in a few weeks."

"So they've got to pull the herb soon or lose it."

"And I have to be tight with Farmer before that happens. I need a lever, and I need it now." He pocketed the camera. "By this time tomorrow I'll have one."

"Damn. You're right, but I still don't like it. Watch your back."

"Don't worry, Mother, I'll be careful." He grinned at Geb's muttered curse.

"Here's your beer." The waitress plunked two bottles on the table. She spun and stomped off, obscenities blistering the air in her wake as the bartender yelled that she should get moving.

Geb shook his head. "Now, is that any way for a lady to talk?" He turned back to Price, face suddenly alight with sly mischief. "Speaking of ladies . . . how goes it with the nosy gym goddess?"

Price actually felt a scowl snap into place. Just thinking about Candy launched a bolt of desire and had his teeth clenching with frustration and something uncomfortably close to panic.

Except for a brief glimpse or two across the crowded gym and a tantalizing brush-by in the doorway of the teachers' lounge, he hadn't seen or touched her for three long days.

He knew why *he* was keeping his distance. He'd given in to the suicidal compulsion to tell her about himself once—damned if he could figure out why—and the urge to open up was still riding him. Sometime during the last seventy-two hours he'd been forced to face the truth: He absolutely hated lying to Candy Johnson.

The reassuring explanation about how he was burned out and tired of lying in general didn't hold water. He wanted to spill his guts only to Candy. That she was somehow more important than everybody else had him backing off as fast as he could.

Unfortunately, the drive to see her, touch her, and taste her more or less balanced out the panic. His libido was playing merry hell with retreat.

Candy's reasons for avoiding *him* remained a mystery. Rabid Curiosity was her middle name; the personal tidbits he'd served up should've only whetted her appetite. So why give him the country-mile routine? It left him torn between relief and resentment.

Damned woman had turned him into a half-wit.

The snapping of dark fingers in front of his face brought him back to Hog Heaven with a start and a blink.

Geb's lips pursed in a soundless whistle. "Man, you have got it bad."

"What?"

"This Candy Johnson must be somethin' else."

"She's something else, all right," Price grumbled, then glowered suspiciously. "What makes you say so?"

"Well," came the drawled reply, "it was probably the way your eyes just kinda *glazed* over when I mentioned her."

"My eyes did not glaze over."

"Trust me, man, glazed *and* dazed. You've got it bad for sure."

"You're not making sense. What have I got?"

"The bug. Never thought I'd see it."

"See what?" For some reason he tensed. His face felt hot. Price scowled. Dammit, he was blushing!

"You. Caught. By a woman."

"I am not caught," Price enunciated carefully.

"Sure you are." Geb sounded gratingly cheerful. His right hand cranked in circles while his left held an imaginary pole. "All she has to do is reel you in."

"Like hell." But he could almost taste the hook. Renewed panic had his temper spiking. "No woman is reeling me anywhere. I'm attracted, that's all."

"Attracted." Geb shook his head in obvious pity. "You're halfway there and don't even know it."

"What are you talking about?"

"Monogamy."

"*Monogamy.*" Stunned by the death-knell ring of truth, Price swallowed heavily. "Damn."

"How'd she do it anyway?"

Raking his fingers through his hair, he swore ripely. "How should I know?" Then, in a last-ditch denial attempt: "She hasn't done anything."

"Uh-huh. So what are you gonna do about it?"

Fight like hell. But the image of himself as a doomed carp was hard to shake. "Look, assuming you were right, which you're not, what do you think I could do about it? I'm there on a job, remember? In a few weeks the buy will be history and I'll be gone. What am I supposed to do—ask her to go with me?"

"Why not?"

"Why not? The woman thinks I'm a gym teacher!"

"Oh, right. Guess she likes the gym-teacher type, huh?" Geb sighed and answered his own question. "Sure she does, she's a gym-teacher type herself."

Amusement trickled into Price's jumbled emotions. "Actually, she wants to be a cop."

"She wants to be a—"

"Cop. Or a PI."

"A cop. Or a PI." Geb stared, and started to chuckle. The chuckle rolled into a belly laugh that had heads turning and Price chortling right along with him. "Damn." Geb sniffed ahead of another chuckle. "Damn, that's rich. A cop."

"You want rich? Check this out: She's a natural."

"No fooling?"

"No fooling." Price's grin tightened. "So what do you think she'll do when she finds out what *I'm* doing? When she finds out why I got close to her in the first place?"

Geb looked cautious. "Well . . . I can't say, seeing as how I never met the lady. What do *you* think she'll do?"

There wasn't a doubt in his mind. "She'll kill me."

A wise man once wrote, "Hell hath no fury like a woman scorned."

Guess again, Will, Candy fumed silently. It was nine A.M. and she was stalking her unsuspecting victim across the gym's hardwood floor because a woman scorned was Little Orphan Annie compared with a would-be seductress foiled.

It wasn't logical, certainly wasn't fair, but somebody was going to pay. She sidled up next to George. Starting now.

"I said a layup, Hamilton! Layup, for God's sake!" George cursed under his breath. "Kid doesn't know his layup from a forward pass," he muttered.

"Hmm." The girls jostled under the basket at one end of the court, the boys at the other. Candy flicked a glance over her shoulder. She and George were alone in this part of the gym with nothing around them but more bleachers.

Stubbornly ignoring her conscience's plea for maturity, she edged closer, pretending to watch the drills as her right hand snaked out to stroke the side of one hairy thigh just below George's red gym shorts. The move was a slow, covert sweep that spelled pure provocation.

He froze. She could almost hear the hum as male nerve endings started to vibrate.

Dizzying power surged through her until she remembered that there was nothing more despicable than a tease. The power surge fizzled. The fact that she'd devolved into a lower life-form almost squelched her irrational desire to get even.

Almost.

"I stopped by your apartment last night," she crooned, and repeated the caress.

"You did?"

"Umm-hmm." The tip of her index finger skimmed under nylon to brush back and forth. "Around nine. You weren't home."

"No. I was—" A quick, sharp breath as a second finger slipped up and under. "Ah . . . out." He cleared his throat. "I was out." He shifted to the right.

She shifted too. "I was *very* disappointed." Her nails scraped lightly, and he jumped.

"What are you—stop that!" he hissed, and stood up on the pretext of calling for free-throw practice.

Standing behind his right shoulder, she murmured under sneaker squeaks and rebounds, "Aren't you going to ask why I stopped by and was disappointed when you weren't there?"

His wary gaze slid back. He studied her face then shook his head and glanced away. "I don't think so."

"But I want to tell you."

"Maybe later. We shouldn't—"

"I went to your place to seduce you."

His head jerked around. He gawked and almost strangled on, "Seduce me?"

Her slow nod and siren's smile reeked of womanly mysteries and sensuality. She knew they did, because she'd perfected them in front of her mirror that morning.

"Oh." His Adam's apple bobbed as he swallowed and swung back toward the court.

Behind his back, her smile twisted with a combination of desire and embarrassment; she felt kind of like a hungry shark with a guilty conscience. But no hint of inner turmoil tainted her soft, longing "I wanted you *so much* last night." It could have steamed paint off walls.

George closed his eyes and muttered something about mercy. Unfortunately for him, she didn't seem to have any.

For the coup de grâce she described, in loving detail, every brief stitch she'd worn the night before. The French-cut panties had his jaw flexing rhythmically. The black lace push-up bra broke him.

Tossing her a wild look and a low growl, he lunged

for a loose basketball. Clutching it in front of his groin, he bellowed hoarsely, "Hit the showers, men!"

And make his subzero. Candy tried, and failed, to convince herself he deserved it. "I hope he chaps."

But the prospect wasn't as gratifying as it should have been. Heaving a dispirited sigh, she went to shepherd her girls off the court.

Rationalization was a losing battle she was still waging hours later.

"You should've been there," she told Columbo, then paused. Heads cocked, they admired her left foot. It was propped on the coffee table; about half of her toes were tipped in Passion's Pink.

"Like I was saying," she continued, dipping the brush again, "you should've been there. I winked at him while he was reffing third period, then slowly ran my tongue over my lips. He almost swallowed his whistle."

Her chuckle sounded weak and annoyed her to no end. Clearing her throat, she continued, "Then I caught him in the library during sixth-period study hall. Full-body brush-and-run right in nonfiction. He snarled."

"*Grrrow.*"

Candy flinched and reluctantly glanced up to find herself skewered on a stern golden glare. "What?" she pouted.

"*Grrrow.*"

Scolded by a cat. Nothing made a woman feel quite so small. "Oh, for—look, he deserved it."

The next low growl underlined a stare of condemnation any hanging judge would envy.

Candy's chagrin simmered for a few seconds before it niggled into full-blown guilt. "Well, maybe I did go overboard. Just a little." She gave it up with a sigh. "Okay, I went overboard a lot. And he didn't deserve a damned thing."

The night before, driven by that blasted pent-up frustration, she'd set off on a course of premeditated seduction. It wasn't George's fault he hadn't been available for assault.

"I was just so mad. Well, not mad, exactly." More like disappointed. "But I shouldn't have taken it out on George. I'll apologize tomorrow, okay?"

Columbo closed his eyes on a satisfied purr.

"Okay." Well, that was certainly a load off her conscience. Just the same . . . "But I really got to him, you know? It was like teasing a caged tiger."

"Is that right?" rumbled a voice.

Her lurch and shriek had Columbo yowling as he launched a low dive for safety. Twisting around to gape at the intruder poised on her threshold, Candy basted her toe and half her instep with Passion's Pink.

One look at George and she knew pink feet would be the least of her problems.

The front door closed behind him. She noticed it vaguely the instant before their gazes locked, which was a split second before she started to babble. "How did you get . . . Where . . . I didn't hear . . ." Oh, boy.

His smile bloomed lazily, showing lots of strong

white teeth, and she went deer-in-the-headlight still. Those gray eyes glinted hungrily.

She'd compared him to a tiger and he was perfectly suited to the role, gliding toward her like a patient hunter on the prowl. Candy didn't need a script to figure out who'd been cast as dinner.

NINE

When a sensible woman finds herself stalked by a large, powerful male wearing a tigerish smile, she should have the sense to panic. She should *not* feel a heady surge of anticipation. Evidently, Candy mused, reports of her sensibleness were greatly exaggerated.

"You little witch." George's voice, deep and dangerously soft, chased a delicious thrill up her spine as she stood.

"Now, George, let's not stoop to name-calling here." She stepped nimbly over the coffee table on the premise that the more obstacles between them, the better. "I'd already decided to apologize. I was out of line today," she admitted, backing away. "I acted like a . . . well, a—"

"A tease?"

Peeved because he hadn't let her off with a palatable euphemism, Candy stopped to sulk. "Yeah." But the truth was a bitter pill to swallow and her jaw set defensively. "So I'm sorry. Okay?"

His stride faltered, and he blinked. Her pugnacious jaw went slack when his ominous smile flashed into a genuine grin. "Okay."

The predator was amused? It caught her off guard until her brain did a conversational replay and she realized that her apology hadn't been what you'd call gracious. Candy wrinkled her nose. "I hate to apologize."

"I noticed." By the time he started toward her again, she was pretty sure life and limb were safe. So when he paused to sweep her into his arms, she decided to relax and enjoy.

Savoring the first lazy stir of arousal, she looped her arms around his neck. "Guess this means you're not mad at me anymore."

He touched a kiss to her lips. "Guess so," he agreed, and started down the hallway. Her pulse skipped a beat then started to race, because it suddenly dawned on her that in a minute she'd have George right where she wanted him.

"Second door on the right," she murmured, nipping lightly at his throat. She felt his arms tighten and smiled.

Pausing in the doorway, he flipped the light switch with his elbow and cleared his throat. "Nice bed."

She forced herself to stop nibbling on him and follow his gaze across the room. Her bed was a queen, cloaked in a flower-strewn comforter, crowned by a mound of ruffled pillows and a scrolled brass headboard. Her eyes widened in abrupt realization. Good grief! Her bed was decadent!

Inexplicably embarrassed, she offered weakly, "I like a lot of room?"

He crossed to the bed and withdrew the arm from under her knees, holding her close while he angled her body for a slow slide down his. He released her and stepped back. "Mmm. That's good, honey, because we're going to need it."

We're going to need it? Suddenly Candy's legs were jelly, clear to her toes, dropping her seat onto the mattress while the air wheezed out of her lungs.

For one breathless moment she wondered if caution wouldn't be the better part of self-preservation after all. Maybe she *was* in too deep and moving way too fast. Then George reached for the buttons on his pinstriped shirt, and she forgot about everything but him.

"Let me," she whispered, and stood. He stilled, his gaze warmed, and he nodded, dropping his hands to his sides. Her unsteady fingers got the job done, and the shirt parted to reveal a tantalizing wedge of hairy chest.

Her low hum was one hundred percent appreciation. She flatted her palms on his stomach, pushed them up and over sculpted muscles and across broad shoulders to sweep the shirt off of his arms. Her hands retraced their path, wrist to shoulder to chest, fingers grazing flat male nipples before they trailed to the snap on his jeans.

"No." One big hand covered hers as he drew a deep breath. "Not yet. Kiss me, Candy."

His free hand tangled in her hair as he bent, urging her up on tiptoe and into his kiss. Their mouths melded, his tongue slid between her lips. He pulled her hands down to cover his erection, groaning deep in his chest when her fingers flexed under his.

Between one heartbeat and the next, the kiss blazed

out of control. Hot, wet, and fierce, his mouth slanted over hers again and again. Drunk on the taste of him, she murmured a protest when he broke off the kiss.

"Give me a minute, sweetheart." He pulled her hands back to his chest, closed his eyes, and dropped back his head. "Just a minute, okay?"

No, it wasn't. But she couldn't drag in the oxygen to tell him so. Judging by the catch in her lungs when he picked her up and laid her on the bed, she might not be able to breathe right anytime soon.

He dropped his glasses onto the nightstand before he stretched out beside her and reached for the first button on her oversized camp shirt. His gaze narrowed on the slender band of skin revealed in the wake of his agile fingers. "No bra?"

His eyes had gone incendiary and ignited fiery tendrils wherever they touched. Candy managed a smile as she lifted a hand to brush his jaw. "I could put one on. The black one."

One long index finger painted heat from her throat to the waistband of her gray leggings. Tracking its leisurely progress, George shook his head. Braced on one elbow, he leaned down to flick his tongue across her lips, his fingers skimming her breasts as they teased and stroked. She gasped against his mouth and clutched at the comforter, already aching for him.

"George," she moaned when he left her lips to trail kisses down her throat and between her breasts. Then his mouth closed over her breast and she gave a sharp, wordless cry as her hands shot up to cradle his head and hold it close. Pleasure washed through her in a warm tide then whipped through her veins as George licked a path to her other breast and slid one heavy leg atop hers.

When his head finally lifted, he was as breathless as she was. The gaze that captured hers could have defrosted Antarctica. The smile that went with it would have brought the place to a full, rolling boil.

"Candy's a good name for you, honey. Sugar sweet," he murmured, and her eyes closed while her heart slammed into her throat.

Her eyes popped open again when he straddled her and slipped his hands under her shoulders to catch the collar of her shirt. He peeled it off and tossed it to the floor. Candy's breath caught as he shifted to the foot of the bed and leaned forward to hook his fingers in the elastic around her waist.

"I've dreamed of seeing you—all of you." He stripped off both leggings and panties in one smooth motion. The belated urge to preserve her modesty was automatic, a fluttery movement of her hands he stopped by saying, "No, don't cover yourself." His eyes lifted to meet hers. "Do you have any idea how beautiful you are?"

So she let him look but couldn't quench the blush kindled by his devouring gaze. Chest rising and falling unevenly, he stood while his eyes swept her with an almost palpable caress.

And in its wake she burned.

He took something out of his pocket before lowering his zipper and stepping out of his jeans.

Her breath developed a serious hitch when George pushed off his snug, maroon jockeys and stood at the foot of the bed. He was magnificent: tall, lean, muscular, and impressively aroused. He protected them both then planted one knee on the mattress and moved to cover her.

Anticipation surged and the need for him swelled. It wouldn't dawn on her until later that the need was bone-deep and much more than physical. Now she could only want.

"Oh, Candy, not yet," he groaned when she reached down to stroke him. His hips shifted away.

She relented, reluctantly withdrawing her hand to wrap her arms around him, giving a shaky sigh when he settled between her legs and came down on top of her.

He levered up on one elbow and stroked a gentle finger down her cheek. "Are you sure?"

"I—" She broke off on a gasp as he moved against her. "I'm sure. Please, George."

"All right, sweetheart. All right." He lowered his head for a kiss as he started to enter. Candy cupped his buttocks and lifted her hips, and suddenly he was fully seated inside her.

"A perfect fit," he whispered, resting his forehead against hers. "I was afraid it would be."

Afraid? There was something wrong with the wording, but Candy was in no condition to critique.

With a sigh that sounded strangely of resignation, he added, "There's only one thing that would make it better." He started to thrust. "This."

When her own hips caught the rhythm he groaned. His fingers speared into her hair as he claimed her mouth for a searing kiss. Waves of sensation rippled out from his every stroke. The pleasure built, a twisting coil of tension so intense, it bordered on pain.

A thought whirled frantically through her mind: Making love with George was more than she'd expected. She was losing herself; she couldn't tell where she ended and he began. A quick sliver of panic arrowed through her because she was feeling too much.

And not enough.

The coil inside her tightened unbearably. "George, I can't—!"

"Yes, you can," he soothed against her lips. "Trust me, Candy. It'll be all right."

The tenderness in his voice dissolved the thin edge of panic, and in that instant tension shattered and ecstasy burst through her. Candy cried out as the universe exploded and consciousness dimmed.

"Yes, honey! Yes!" he moaned, and thrust into her. The first wave of rapture had barely ebbed when she was submerged in another.

The second trip to heaven was even more overwhelming than the first. And this time she took George with her.

He'd probably been crushing her for some time, but there was no way in hell he could move yet. Completely exhausted, Price rested atop Candy's perspiration-soaked body.

She didn't seem to notice his weight but lay in a contented sprawl beneath him, one hand stroking the small of his back. He felt as well as heard her quiet sigh of satisfaction.

Ideally he'd still be inside her and stay there until he grew hard and they made love again. But he'd withdrawn immediately, resenting for the first time the limitations imposed by safe sex.

Candy stirred languidly. "You're an amazing man, George Price."

"Damn straight," he mumbled into her hair. Then, with a little more interest: "Why?"

"I came."

"I noticed."

She sighed again. "Amazing." Turning, she draped a leg across his thighs and fit her curves against his side. Her fingers toyed with the hair on his chest.

He lifted his head to look at her. No way she could mean . . . "Your first?"

The answer was a small, cat-that-ate-the-canary smile. "Umm-hmm."

It didn't make sense. The woman was a blonde, blue-eyed powder keg. "You weren't a virgin."

She snorted. "Neither were you."

"But . . ." He raked a hand through his hair. "I don't get it."

"Well, I am kind of new at this."

For some reason his heart started to pound. "Define *new at this.*"

"What?"

"How many times have you . . . uh . . ." He trailed off, totally discomfited by the abrupt discovery that he was embarrassed to ask.

"Hmm. Let's see." Silence. "There was one guy. In college."

"And?"

"And that's it. I didn't see what all the fuss was about. Until now."

Price closed his eyes. Dear God, she hadn't made love with a man in . . . too damned long. Rolling onto his side, he studied her face. Calm, contented, and slightly smug.

"You keep surprising me," he murmured, reaching up to stroke a finger through her damp bangs.

Her gaze was warm and amused. "And you don't like surprises?"

"I don't know. I haven't decided."

"Let me know when you make up your mind," she suggested, and stretched languidly, kindling a spark of interest that had his eyes widening in surprise. Already? Damn! "How do I keep surprising you?"

"What? Oh." He tried to think beyond the fact that, impossibly, he wanted her again. "I thought I had you pegged. A dumb jockette with more—ouch!" He slapped a hand over hers before she could pull his chest hair again.

Candy gave him a mild look as her fingers moved under his, stroking now. "I am not a dumb jockette."

"I know that now, but finding out was a surprise. And you just keep springing them on me," he muttered. "Like your family, the fact that you want to be a cop. Then there were the looks," he said, remembering her courtside seduction routine. His blood heated in response.

"What looks?"

"You know what looks," he growled, and leaned in for a quick, hard kiss. "Hot enough to . . . Dammit, woman, you drove me crazy all day long! And now I find out that you're almost an innocent."

"Almost an innocent," she reminded him as her hand skated down his belly, "doesn't count."

"It does too. Why—" He broke off, unsure of what he wanted to ask. Why me? Why now? The answers struck him as vital, but her fingers wrapped around him and all of a sudden he was too hard to hold on to the questions. "I wanted to know—"

Candy huffed impatiently. "Do we have to talk about this right now?"

Her foot glided up his calf and Price swallowed heavily. Agitation and arousal were a potent combination. Unable to form another coherent thought, he croaked, "No. Not right now."

"Good." She pushed him over onto his back and bent down to tease his lips with hers. "I have a question."

"What?" Her caressing hand had him hooking an arm around her neck to pull her down for a real kiss.

When it was over she trailed her mouth down his throat. Against his skin she murmured, "Can I be on top this time?"

So much for the pent-up-frustration theory.

Lying on her back with one arm crooked under her head, Candy studied George by the watery light of a storm-drenched dawn. He slept facing her on his side, blankets twisted around his hips, one arm draped across her waist, one heavy leg thrown over both of hers.

Contrary to several romance novels she'd read, her hero didn't look young or boyish or gentled by sleep. His angular jaw was shadowed with blue-black bristle.

He looked big and tough and kind of . . . well, dangerous. Remembering their night of heated lovemaking, she sighed.

Oh, George was dangerous, all right.

She'd have to wake him soon—from across the room, of course. Kissing him awake held definite appeal, but then they'd never get to school on time. If they got there at all, she admitted, and grinned.

The grin faded as her gaze shifted to the rain-spattered window. Waking George would have to wait until she came to grips with the truth that had crept up on her sometime between the middle of the night and sudden, wide-eyed wakefulness.

She loved him.

There was no denying the obvious. After last night the pent-up-frustration theory didn't hold water, mainly because after last night she didn't *have* any pent-up frustration.

No, she loved him. Which was really too bad, she mused wistfully. Frustration would have been easier to live with. She didn't want to be in love. It was the wrong time, and George was the wrong kind of man. Unfortunately, neither of those things seemed to matter.

Loving George could mean giving up all her plans and dreams. Granted, he'd encouraged her to go for those dreams, but they hadn't been lovers at the time. Assuming her feelings were returned—a risky assumption to make based on one night of lovemaking—he might change his mind. Most men wouldn't want the woman they love in the line of fire.

Her brow furrowed thoughtfully. Another twenty

or so years of teaching loomed as a distinct possibility. Surely that deserved a shudder or two, a goodly dose of regret. So where were they?

Nonexistent, she realized with a slow smile. Because George was all the intrigue and excitement she could want or handle. In exchange for his love, she'd gladly endure twenty years of lesson plans and several generations of grudging student participation.

Still smiling, she looked back at George and shook her head. Yep, she loved him. From the top of his greasy head to the soles of his imitation-leather running shoes. He might be a nerd but he was *her* nerd, and she'd personally flay the skin off anybody who uttered one word against him.

Her gaze slid past him to the chunky glasses lying on her nightstand. *Just look at those lenses. Poor baby. He's as blind as a bat.*

Moving cautiously so as not to wake him, Candy levered herself up on an elbow, reached across his body, and picked up the glasses. Just how strong was his prescription?

Handling George's glasses felt incredibly intimate. She relished the sense of connection as warmth spread through her. Raising the glasses to her eyes, she had to resist a giddy urge to laugh out loud.

Fixing her gaze on the O'Keeffe print on the opposite wall, she peered through the lenses and waited for the lush flower to bleed into a colorful blur. When that didn't happen she closed her eyes. Opened them, slowly, and looked again.

The print remained stubbornly and bewilderingly in focus.

Confused and fighting a mounting sense of dread, Candy sat up carefully, perched the glasses on her nose, and did a desperate sweep of the room. Her frantic gaze bounced from object to object. Everything she saw, she saw with vicious, crystal clarity.

Everything. Including the fact that she'd been a complete and utter fool.

Oh, God.

Betrayal was icy, a creeping cold that froze heart and soul. Some distant voice warned that pain would explode when shock thawed, blasting the ice into blue-hot flame. But now there was only merciful numbness.

Candy dragged off the glasses and dropped them into her lap. Her eyes, so dry they ached, locked compulsively on the face of the man sleeping next to her. Last night she'd given herself to him body, mind, and soul.

And she didn't know who he was.

TEN

"Candy?" George rubbed a hand over her shoulder.

Don't touch me! She almost screamed it. Blessed shock had long since worn off, and his caress gave razor edges to relentless waves of pain. Clenching her teeth against the cry that threatened to boil up her throat, Candy kept her face buried in the pillow, giving what she hoped sounded like a sleepy mutter of protest.

"Sweetheart? Wake up for just a minute, okay?"

His hand. She couldn't bear it. The same slow stroke had brushed waves of pleasure over her last night; now it threatened to tear her apart. Desperate to escape both the sensation and her agonizing memories, she mumbled, "No," and squirmed away like a determined sleeper.

New anguish raked through her as she wondered if she'd ever sleep again without dreaming of him.

"All right." He murmured it so tenderly. Her eyes, tightly shut, started to burn. "You go ahead and sleep. I've got to go or one of your neighbors will catch me leaving and give old Mrs. Bimson a field day. I'll see you later, honey."

His lips whispered over her hair and pushed the first tear through her eyelids. Another squeezed through after it, and another, until a silent stream soaked the pillow.

Go. Please go now. Her fingers gripped the pillow tightly as she listened. Footsteps in the hallway, a muffled word to Columbo, the quiet sound of the front door as it closed.

Finally, the first ragged sob tore up her throat.

Stupid: to fall for a lying, sneaking SOB with a windowpane eyeglass prescription. *Radically stupid:* to stand across the street from his apartment at eleven o'clock on a stormy October night, crying your eyes out while the cold rain ran off your hooded slicker and rivered into your boots.

Candy decided that achieving radical stupidity was the perfect end to an absolute horror of a day.

How she'd gotten through the dragging, pain-filled hours was anyone's guess. She felt battered and bruised, pummeled by the twin fists of fury and despair. She'd cried through a shower, an uneaten breakfast, and the drive to work, barely managing to get herself under control and wash her tearstained face before anyone saw her.

Why did he lie to me? Why did he make love to me? Who is he? What am I going to do now? But while the questions tormented, the answers eluded.

She'd fallen apart again at lunchtime in the privacy

of her office situated just off the gym. She remembered the hubbub streaming through the door behind her—girlish voices, running water, and slamming lockers. It seemed oddly distant as she stood in the opposite doorway, staring across the gym at the dirty, low-down rat who'd broken her heart.

He'd been coaching Danny Barns, a sweet fifteen-year-old with a problematic jump shot. When Danny finally swished one through the net, George whooped and shared a triumphant high five. His exuberance shattered her thin shield of composure. She barely managed to close her office door before she dissolved into racking sobs.

She'd pulled herself back together and toughed out the rest of the day on sheer, stubborn pride, only to cry herself into near dehydration again at home. Her emotions continued to swing wildly from bleak sorrow to coruscating rage and back again.

But now she started to think.

A few truths had been scattered among the lies. George loved classic rock, hated rules, and had overcome a lousy childhood. Most important, he'd made love to her with a passion that couldn't be faked.

Gradually, she'd come to the confusing conclusion that George didn't *want* to lie to her. Wishful thinking? She didn't think so, not when she looked back on all those times she'd poked and prodded only to find herself kissed questionless. Whenever possible, George chose avoidance and distraction over deceit.

So here she stood, a sniveling idiot dressed for rain and mourning in her black sweats and navy slicker, dithering over what to do about George. Her inclination wavered between direct confrontation and outright murder.

"He's probably in there getting ready to sleep like a baby," she muttered, and dabbed at her tender nose with a soggy wad of Kleenex. "No-good lying snake."

The lights in his apartment winked out, apparently confirming her suspicions, and Candy's mood veered toward homicidal. Then the door opened and George stepped out. She edged back between Mr. Butler's prize lilacs, too busy gawking to realize she'd automatically hidden herself.

He paused in the halo of the porch light to scan the street, an imposing figure dressed in black from his jeans and what looked like a heavy black turtleneck to his black vinyl poncho. His thick, wavy hair was tousled by the wind until he pulled up his hood.

Needless to say, he'd ditched the glasses.

Casting one last twenty-twenty look around, he started up the walk, his long-legged stride quick and purposeful. Finding it hard to believe that this fierce-looking stranger could be the same gorgeous dweeb she'd made love with last night, she stared after him.

Whoever, *whatever* George Price was, he was no nerd. He was quick, strong, and competent.

The slimy, rotten louse.

And the louse was up to something.

Candy intended to find out just what that something was. Lips firming with determination, she knuckled the tears out of her eyes, squared her shoulders, and followed him.

❖────────❖

Price ghosted around the corner of Main and Pine with an almost imperceptible shrug, but the prickle between his shoulder blades stuck like a burr. He would have sworn he was being followed, but he knew better and squelched the urge to glance over his shoulder again. He'd only see the same nothing he'd seen the last three times he'd stopped to look.

As he left the center of town the glow of streetlights dwindled to a weak pool on the occasional corner, shrinking visibility to near zero. Price nodded with satisfaction. The cover provided by this miserable night more than made up for being cold and wet.

Actually, he mused with a wry grimace, since memories of Candy clinging to him while he plunged into her sweet, wet heat kept sneaking into his head to make him hard, cold and wet were good points.

One night in her bed had wrought havoc with his famed powers of concentration. He shook his head, scowling in exasperation. *Get a grip, dammit! You've got a job to do.*

He picked up his pace and turned right onto Horseshoe Bar. Setting his jaw, he forcibly evicted fantasies about a maddening blonde. A man needed a cool head for B and E.

"Oh, my God!"

The truth was much worse than she'd imagined. Candy crouched under Ethel May Farmer's boisterous tangle of forsythia, horrified witness to the start of what promised to be a well-planned and flawlessly executed felony.

lashed rain against the windows. Mother Nature wasn't the only one who was ticked off.

"Why the hell does he bother to lock the damned desk? Nobody's going to steal this trash."

Another antsy tickle crawled up his spine and he whirled, coming face-to-face with an empty room. Jaw clenched, he stole silently over to the door to look into an equally empty hallway. Groaning softly, he moved back to the desk.

"I'm losing my mind and my instincts are off. We all know whose fault that is." But he'd deal with her later.

He reached into the drawer again, his fingers closed around a familiar shape, and he froze. Expression grim, he lifted the pistol and stared. Turned it over in his hand, frowned, and stared some more.

Then he chuckled. "I'll be damned."

Pointing the weapon heavenward, he slowly squeezed the trigger. A tiny flame flickered from the muzzle and he grinned, uncurling his finger as his gaze fell back to the drawer and caught on a check stub. Eyes narrowed, he leaned closer, picked up the stub, and straightened. Payable to Duff Farmer, the check had been issued by Grass Roots Agri-Con, Incorporated.

Price smiled with satisfaction. "Bingo."

The roar of her heartbeat filled the cramped hiding place. Candy sucked in a shaky breath and let it out slowly, closing her eyes. That had been too damned close.

If George hadn't warned her by going completely still for a second or two, he would have caught her gaping in the doorway as he rifled through Duff's desk. As it was, she was pretty sure *barely made it* characterized her duck into the hall closet. Now she had to work up the nerve to open the door and walk out again so she could save the big jerk from himself.

She could see it now and all too clearly: George sneering out the window as he taunted Hiram Walters à la James Cagney. "Forget it, copper, you'll never take me alive!"

Her jaw set with renewed resolve.

Damn right he won't take you alive, she fumed as she carefully opened the door. She was the one who loved him, the one he'd hurt the most with his lies. Miserable creep. She swiped impatiently at a new batch of tears and made herself a fierce promise. If anybody was going to off George Price, it was going to be her.

Cradling the heavy skillet against her stomach, she glided toward the soft spill of light at the end of the hall. With a nervous lick of her lips she stepped boldly but quietly into the doorway, creeping up behind the figure bent over the desk.

"Bingo," he said softly, and scratched his chin.

With the barrel of his gun.

Freezing in her tracks, Candy goggled. Her mouth went dry, her palms clammy. He had a gun.

A shocked second later her mind started to work again, furiously. Gun plus robbery equals . . . armed robbery! Ten to twenty in San Quentin. Providing he didn't get shot first.

Her eyes narrowed on his unsuspecting back as a

fresh wave of wrath all but sent steam shooting out of her ears. The big, stupid idiot!

Her lips clamped on a violent oath as she changed her grip, wrapping all ten fingers around the skillet's handle. Two quick, silent steps put her directly behind him.

This is going to hurt you a lot more than it does me. The thought had her battling a potent surge of guilt as she raised her arms.

George stiffened.

She clobbered him before he could so much as turn his head.

It is definitely time to look for another line of work, Price decided groggily.

He latched onto the beginnings of consciousness like a dog would his last bone, and bit back a moan. Not that he wasn't entitled to a moan or two; pain knifed through his skull with every heartbeat. But until he cleared up a couple of minor points, like where he was and who'd gotten the drop on him, he'd damn well stay "out cold."

Soft fingers stroked the hair off his forehead. "George? I'd really appreciate it if you'd wake up now."

His heart lurched wildly. What was Candy doing here? Had they taken her too?

Self-protection was forgotten; Price's eyes snapped open, blinking her pale, worried face into focus. He was stunned to realize she'd been crying. From fear?

For him? Regret and guilt tore at his conscience. "Oh, baby, I'm so sorry."

The hand he tried to lift to her cheek wouldn't budge, a fact that had him jerking his head off the floor and gaping from his bound hands to his equally bound feet. Both appeared to be wrapped in a couple of miles of fuzzy red yarn.

He stared. *Yarn?*

"You're not," Candy promised in ominous tones, "as sorry as you're going to be."

The switch from tender to threatening didn't surprise him. Not that he hadn't been known to think fast in tight spots, but even a moron could add up these facts: Angry woman, red-yarn manacles, and a major-league goose egg courtesy of the cast-iron skillet lying beside him on the floor of Farmer's study.

He was in big trouble.

He tried a placating smile. "Listen, honey, I can explain." He just had to figure out the what and how.

"Oh, you're going to explain, George." She paused. "That *is* your name, isn't it?" Her gaze probed his face then slid away filled with . . . *pain?* "I see. What is your real name?"

He'd hurt her. The unexpected knowledge tore at him. "I can't tell you that."

Her spine went rigid and her eyes whipped back to his face. Rage, he thought, relieved. The gaze that slashed at him simmered with it. Thank God. He'd take her temper over her pain any day.

"Oh, you're going to tell me. Damn menace." She scooted around to sit facing him. "Everything. And after I've heard your rap sheet, in detail, we'll decide."

"Rap sheet?" He blinked. She must have walloped him a good one; it would explain why his hearing was scrambled. "Decide?"

"Whether to stay put or leave the country." She stabbed a finger at his nose. "Listen up, Mr. whatever your damned name is, because I've got a news flash for you. You are going straight. Right now, tonight. Clear?"

"Huh?"

She nodded. "Not clear. Okay," she said, bending down, "read my lips. From this day forward you will not break and enter." She held up the lighter. "You will not commit armed robbery. Dammit, George, I don't want to see so much as a parking ticket against you. Got it?"

His jaw dropped as he shook his head. "You think I'm a thief?"

"Were. You were a thief. Not anymore." Her eyes narrowed. "Isn't that right?"

He couldn't help it, he laughed. It exploded from his chest, an unstoppable gale of mirth that made his ribs ache and his eyes water. Candy's expression went from nonplussed to suspicious to hopping mad. She reached for the frying pan.

"Wait," he gasped, choking on his fight for control. "Let me explain."

"Go ahead. I'm waiting."

"It's not—" He gulped air. "I'm not what you think I am."

"You don't want to know what I think you are right now," she said, brandishing the skillet. "You broke into the Farmers' house."

"Yes, but not because I want to steal anything. I'm no thief."

"Then what, exactly, are you?"

The urge to laugh evaporated because there was nothing funny about trusting someone with your life. "I need to know that you won't repeat anything I'm about to tell you."

"You aren't, by any chance, asking if *you* can trust *me*, are you, George?" Her voice was dead soft, edged with accusation, and he flinched.

If he didn't talk fast she'd bash him again. "I'm with the DEA."

"The DEA?" Candy repeated stupidly.

"Drug Enforcement Agency."

"I know what it means," she muttered, eyeing him sourly. He was disheveled, pale, trussed like a turkey in Ethel May's knitting yarn . . . and he was still absolutely gorgeous. Too bad she didn't dare trust him. "So you're, what? An agent?"

"Special agent." His weak grin was an obvious hint to lighten up. It only made her want to hit him again.

"Prove it."

His grin collapsed. "I can't."

"Sure you can. Show me your badge."

"I don't carry a badge when I'm working under-cover."

"Undercover." She shook her head, suddenly feeling miserable again. "I don't know you at all, do I? I made love with you, and I don't even know your name."

"I didn't want to lie to you," he said brusquely.

"Believe it or not, I already figured that out." But hearing him say so soothed the ache a little.

"I'd tell you my name if I could. But it'll be easier for you to play along with my cover if you don't know it."

"I see what you mean." Taking a deep breath, she pinned him with a stern glare. "Okay, we'll let the name business slide. For now. Let's talk about something else, like since when the DEA goes in for housebreaking. Or do you have a warrant?"

He grimaced. "No," he admitted, "no warrant. This visit is strictly unofficial."

"One could even say illegal."

"I'm a fed, remember? I know the law." He winced, shifted impatiently, and lifted his hands. "Look, why don't you untie me? After I get the information I came for, we'll go back to your place. I'll swallow a bottle or two of aspirin, and we'll talk."

"We'll talk now." She would *not* feel sorry for him. After what he'd put her through, a headache was the least he deserved. "How do I know you're telling the truth?"

"You think I'm lying to you?" He sounded so completely insulted that her lips twitched in spite of her unhappiness.

"It's been known to happen."

He blinked, then looked sheepish. "Oh. I, uh, see what you mean."

"Um-hmm. So maybe you should tell me about this information you came for."

"Stubborn woman." His eyes closed. "I think I

dropped it on the desk right before you gave me that cast-iron crack on the skull. Look for a check stub. Damn, but my head aches."

"You'll live," she muttered, straining guilt and sympathy out of her voice as she climbed to her feet. "Unless you lie to me again."

"I knew you were a dangerous woman."

"Keep it in mind." The check stub was exactly where he said it would be. Candy studied it, frowning thoughtfully. "So this is where Duff gets his money." She glanced down to find George watching her through slitted eyes. "Grass Roots Agri-Con, Incorporated. What's that?"

"They call themselves an agricultural conglomerate." She raised an eyebrow. "Weed, baby. Grass Roots grows and sells high-grade Colombian. They're smart and slick and raking in the profits. We want them out of business and off the streets."

She shot him a disbelieving look. "You think Duff Farmer is a drug pusher?"

George shook his head. "He probably doesn't know what's going on. Chances are, he leased them the land in good faith. It happens all the time. Even if Farmer bothered to drive out for a look-see, I doubt he'd look past the corn."

"But you did."

"Yeah." He watched her closely, and she knew he was waiting for her decision.

Candy hesitated. Would she be a fool to believe him? Probably, but she didn't seem to have a choice. With a mental sigh she laid down the check stub, knelt beside him, and went to work on the labyrinth of fuzzy knots. "So what happens now?"

"SOP, standard operating procedure," he explained, "would be to torch this field like we did the last fifteen." When his wrists were free he sat up, rubbing the back of his head while she struggled with the yarn around his ankles.

"So why haven't you?"

"We don't want to close the net on this bunch until we can catch all the fish."

"You're going to set up an ambush."

He stood and reached down to tug her up beside him. "You'll make one hell of a cop, sweetheart. I told Geb you were a natural."

Forget the compliments, buster, you're not out of the doghouse yet. Candy ruthlessly quashed the traitorous glow his words gave her. "Geb?"

"Jamal Gebhardt, my partner."

"Oh." Standing behind his shoulder, she watched him pull out a tricky little camera and snap a picture of the check stub. "Why don't you just take it with you?"

"I don't want to spook Farmer."

"But you said he didn't know what was going on."

George shook his head and tidied up the desk. "I said he *probably* doesn't know what's going on." He glanced at the gun she held and extended his hand, palm up, cocking an expectant brow.

Candy surrendered the automatic, gaping when he tossed it carelessly into the drawer. "That was *Duff's* gun?"

"No." He closed the drawer and switched off the lamp, plunging the room into darkness. His hand closed around hers. "That was Duff's cigarette lighter."

"Oh." She let him tow her through the house, wondering when he'd add up the facts and realize that she'd given him a mild concussion because he'd been carrying an unconcealed lighter.

"So what happens now?" she asked as he relocked the kitchen door. She had to raise her voice to be heard over the wind and rain.

"The stub is a lever." He grabbed her hand again and pulled her across the lawn. "Farmer's due back in town tomorrow or the next day. We'll confront him with it and see which way he jumps."

She struggled to match his long strides. "You're going to interrogate Duff?"

"Not me, Geb. I'm undercover, remember?"

"Oh. Right."

Falling silent, they hurried forward, shoulders hunched against the biting storm-whipped night as they headed toward her apartment. Candy's thoughts raced as quickly as her feet as she tried to assimilate the day's astounding chain of revelations.

She loved a man, but she didn't know his name. He'd lied to her but said it was part of his job. He was here now but would no doubt leave when the job was done.

All of which left her with two thorny problems. One, she had to decide whether or not to trust him again. Two, trust him or not, she had to convince him to take her along when he left Donnerton.

Because whoever and whatever he was, she didn't think she could let him go.

ELEVEN

"Damn!" Price winced as he gingerly fingered the swelling at the back of his head. He stomped into Candy's cheery yellow-and-white kitchen and stood in the doorway wearing a towel and a scowl. "You could have fractured my skull with that frying pan."

She lounged against the counter, studying him over the rim of her coffee cup. "Did I?"

"No." He touched the lump again and grimaced. "But not for lack of trying."

"Don't be such a big baby. Let me see." She stepped behind him, and he caught a whiff of flowers as her fingers gently parted his hair. "Hmm. The skin's not broken, but maybe we should have Doc Shay check you out just to be on the safe side."

He knew she'd gone on tiptoe to look, because her breasts skimmed his back. Given the way his body reacted to the scent and feel of her, any discussion about possible head injuries would be a short one. Well, he could hope anyway.

Clearing his throat, he said, "No doctor."

"But—"

"Do you want to be the one who explains how I came by this particular bump?"

"Oh." Her fingers left his hair. He stifled a sigh of regret as she came to stand in front of him and a tortured groan when she nibbled her lower lip. She always did that when she thought, and it always drove him crazy. "We could improvise an explanation. That lump should be looked at."

"I'm fine."

"No double vision? Nausea?" she asked when he shook his head.

"Nope."

"Trembling?"

He started to tell her no again but paused. "Well, now that you mention it, I do feel kind of weak and shaky."

"You do?" She peered anxiously into his eyes. "Your pupils look okay."

"Are you sure?" He settled his hands on her waist and pulled her close.

"Yes, I—" Her eyebrows snapped together as her gaze dropped to where blue satin met white terry cloth. She looked back at him, a kind of you're-hopeless expression on her face.

He searched for a smile but couldn't find it in him, because there was just too much on the line. Had she forgiven him? Would she ever trust him again?

The answer to at least one of his questions dawned in her eyes, and he knew she wouldn't turn him down tonight. Relief coursed through him as he grinned, bent at the waist, and tossed her over his shoulder.

"Kind of weak and shaky? I ought to whack you another one," she decided, and pinched his butt.

"Forget it. You had your shot, babe. I can't understand how you got the drop on me in the first place."

"Caught you flat-footed, didn't I?" For a woman who was hanging upside down, she sounded awfully proud of herself. "A gift for surveillance, that's what I've got. Followed you from your apartment to the Farmers', and you didn't spot me once."

Realization slapped him to a standstill next to the bed. "I'll be—" he breathed. "You did, didn't you? I didn't even think about that."

"Not bad, huh?"

"No," he gritted, "not bad." He swore viciously and at length. "Stupid. You little idiot! What in the hell did you think you were doing?"

"What? I—hey!" He tossed her onto the bed; she bounced once, sat up, and glared. "Just what is your problem, anyway?"

"*My* problem?" He dragged in a breath, searching for an ounce of patience. "You followed me tonight."

Her chin lifted as she folded her arms. "Obviously. So?"

"Alone."

"Uh-huh. I repeat, so?"

"You want *so*? I'll give you *so*. You followed a man you suspected of—" He broke off to frown. "What did you suspect me of?"

Her face lost some of its belligerence. "Everything." She shrugged. "Nothing. I knew only that you weren't what you claimed to be."

"How did you know that?"

"I looked through your glasses."

And found herself in bed with an impostor. Imagining how she must have felt, he winced. "I'm sorry you had to find out that way, honey. I would've told you the truth eventually."

"You would have?"

Stung by her wide-eyed surprise, he glowered. "Damn right I would have."

"Oh."

She smiled and reached for him, but as much as he wanted her, he forced himself to step back. "I'm not through with this discussion."

"You're not?" She sighed. "Oh, I get it. Okay, I'm sorry I hit you. Well, mostly. I was steamed."

The sheer magnitude of her recklessness slammed home again and he growled. "Yeah, steamed senseless. You knew I'd lied about who I was, and you followed me anyway. Alone and unarmed, down dark streets to a deserted house." He pinned her with a look. "Then what happened?"

Her eyes rolled as she replied with exaggerated obedience, "I saw you break in."

"You saw me break in." His jaw clenched. "And instead of calling the cops, you did what?"

Her eyes narrowed. "What is this, a quiz? You know damned well what I did."

"Humor me," he forced himself to say through gritted teeth.

Through her own gritted teeth: "I slipped in after

you. It suddenly occurred to me that you might be armed, so I grabbed a skillet. Then I went looking for you."

"You thought you could take out an armed man with a frying pan? You're certifiable, you know that?"

"Oh, yeah?" she snarled, surging to her knees. "Guess again, pal. I *did* take out an armed man with a frying pan!"

"I wasn't armed!"

"I didn't know that, you jackass! This is all your fault anyway," she yelled, springing to her feet to meet him toe-to-toe. "I wouldn't have had to follow you if you'd told me what was going on!"

Her skin was flushed, her blue eyes glittered, her breasts heaved. She was magnificent. He wanted her, needed her like he'd never needed a woman. *What would he have done if something had happened to her?*

Fear, rage, lust, and an emotion he couldn't name roiled together, an explosive brew that had him shouting in her face, "It was a damned-fool thing to do, and you know it! You could have been killed! And for what? Why the hell would you pull a boneheaded stunt like that?"

Her fist waved in his face. "I'll tell you why, you sneaky, low-down, lying phony! Because I love you, that's why!"

Shocked silence pierced by a single, quickly caught breath. His or hers? All but drowning in her horrified gaze, he swallowed. "Come again?" he croaked.

She stared up at him and moistened her lips. "You want me to repeat the part about you being a sneaky, low-down, lying phony?" He shook his head and one corner of her mouth crooked ruefully. "I didn't think so."

His hands lifted involuntarily, wrapping themselves around her upper arms. Emotions tangled in his chest, the knot so thick and tight it hurt to breathe. "Candy?"

Her half smile melted as she reached up to cup his face. He read it in her eyes, then heard her say it. "I love you."

The words winded him, freezing his next breath. His heart pounded as thoughts tumbled wildly through his head. She loved him. Nobody had ever said that to him before. He should thank her. Tell her he felt . . . what? Too much, he realized suddenly. Too fast and all at once. Which left him with only one alternative.

"Come here, sweetheart," he groaned, pulled her into his arms, and kissed her. He meant to be tender, but his emotions clawed free and control shredded.

Her arms wound around his neck as she went up on her toes, straining against him, eagerly accepting his tongue. *Too sweet*, he wanted to tell her. *Too hot. You're burning me alive.* But he couldn't tear himself away from her mouth.

His hands skimmed down then up and under her nightshirt to grip the smooth, firm curves of her buttocks. He tugged, molding her to his erection and groaned again when she circled her hips.

"I can't wait," he rasped against her lips. "I'm sorry, baby, but I need you now."

"Yes, now." Unwinding her arms from around his neck, she stepped back, and holding his gaze with her own, quickly stripped the nightshirt off over her head.

His hungry eyes devoured her as she reached for his

towel. He cupped her breasts, watching her nipples harden under twin strokes of his thumbs. The towel dropped away, he wrapped her in his arms, and toppled them both onto the bed.

He slipped on one of the condoms he'd dropped on the nightstand earlier then pulled her underneath him, spreading her thighs with his own as he came down on top of her and slid inside. Perfect. Absolutely perfect, he thought, and paused, gritting his teeth. Still staring into her eyes, he started to move. Her hips rose to meet his steady thrusts, her hands clutched his upper arms.

"Candy, you feel like—" *Home* he almost said, but her lips found his and the half-formed thought scattered.

The kiss staggered him. It was as if she wanted to pour herself into him, heart and soul; it was a gift and he couldn't, wouldn't refuse it. Slanting his mouth over hers, he drank greedily.

Finally, her head dropped back onto the pillow. Lips parted, breath choppy, she moved with him, still grasping his arms, watching his face as he rocked into her. "I love you," she said again, and something inside him snapped.

Reclaiming her mouth, he drove into her over and over. She met him thrust for thrust, accepting him with a hot, slick generosity that blew what was left of his mind.

He lifted his head to look into blue eyes gone hazy with passion. "Wrap those beautiful legs around me, sweetheart."

She smiled. Her legs slid around him, sleek and strong, her ankles locked at the small of his back. And she pulled him in. Deeper. She raised her arms, lightly clasping her hands at the back of his neck.

"Kiss me," she murmured, pulling down his head. "Kiss me again, George."

Her eyes held both a dare and a promise, and his heart hammered even harder as he groaned and crushed her mouth. He plunged deep—once, twice, three times—and she came, crying into his mouth as the lightning contractions gripped them both, tearing a low moan from deep in his chest as he surged into her one last time.

Later they lay side by side, breathless, exhausted, their bodies filmed with sweat. Somehow he mustered the strength to pull her into his arms, but he still felt dazed and wrung out.

It had been one hell of a night.

First Candy knocked him cold, then she had him spilling his beans all over Farmer's study. She jumped into a rousing argument with both feet only to stop it dead with a stunning declaration. Then to top it all off, she took him on a headfirst couple's dive into oblivion. One way or another his lady would be the death of him.

His eyes drifted shut, and he smiled.

Three A.M. and she still hadn't decided. Either she'd taken a giant step forward when she told George she loved him . . . or she'd cut her throat. Blank amazement, confusion, and raw desperation—did this add up to a positive reaction? She just didn't know.

At least he didn't run screaming into the night.

Whether or not he ran screaming into the sunrise remained to be seen.

A muscled thigh brushed her legs as George shifted. "Can't sleep?" he rumbled quietly.

She angled her head, trying to see his face. "I'm sorry, I didn't mean to wake you."

"You didn't. I was just lying here, thinking."

"Me too."

His arm, draped across her waist, tucked her closer. "What about?"

"Where do we go from here?" she blurted, and closed her eyes. Damn. A woman shouldn't ask relationship questions until she was sure she'd get answers she could live with.

"What do you mean?" he asked slowly.

Since it was too late to clap a hand over her mouth, Candy did some quick thinking. "Your investigation. Where do we go from here?" Was it her imagination, or did his arm relax?

"*We* don't go anywhere. I'll call Geb in the morning and start the wheels of justice turning. The rest depends on what he gets from Farmer."

I'm not letting you out of my sight, buster, was something she wasn't dumb enough to say out loud. "You've been working on this a long time, haven't you?"

"A couple of years."

"You're kidding! *Years?*"

Her head rested on his shoulder, so she felt the shrug. "I've been on longer assignments."

"Undercover?"

"Yeah, some."

"I wouldn't have expected the DEA to invest that

much time and manpower to track down a ring of mar-
ijuana growers. Cocaine traffickers, maybe. But most
kids—most adults, for that matter—consider pot pretty
mild. Kind of like a couple of beers."

"It used to be. But today's stuff is strong, and the
pleasant buzz is yesteryear's news."

"A lot of people think it should be legalized."

"Maybe. But until and unless it is, it's part of the
job."

"Do you like your job?"

Silence, and the absent stroke of his hand over her
hip. Then: "I used to. Growing up where I did gives
you an up-close and personal view of what drugs can do
to people, a neighborhood, a city. I was fresh out of
college when I signed up to fight that war. Seemed like
a good idea at the time. But to tell you the truth, lately
I've thought about resigning."

Candy turned on her side. They hadn't gotten
around to turning off the lights in the living room, so
she could make out his shadowed profile. She laid a
hand on his chest. "Tell me why."

He shrugged again. "Frustration, for one thing.
Undercover assignments can be long and dangerous.
Years of painstaking effort that may or may not result
in a bust. If you're lucky and nobody messes up on the
technicalities, you might even get a conviction.

"But for every dealer we put away, there are ten
more waiting to take his place.

"Then there's the work itself. Deep cover can be a
trap. You act like scum and you live with scum. If the
assignment goes on long enough, your perspective gets
warped, because you've been living with these guys,

working with them. You start to think maybe they're not so bad after all. That's why you've got a partner who stays outside; he reminds you of who and what you are. Who and what *they* are.

"Then one day you wake up and realize you've been living one lie after another, laying your butt on the line and wallowing in filth while the bureaucracy that's supposed to back you up chokes on its own red tape." He paused and snorted, his grin sardonic. "The sob story of the burned-out narco, baby."

He was tired and disillusioned, and she ached for him. But he wouldn't welcome her sympathy, so she slid her arms around his neck and planted a kiss on his jaw. "Sounds like we both need a career change."

"Yeah." He looked at her and cocked an eyebrow. "But I thought you'd plotted yours out. You want to be a cop, remember?"

Candy wrinkled her nose. "Not if I have to wade through a sea of technicalities and red tape. Besides, if my dealings with Arvin Carmichael are any indication, bureaucrats give me a rash. Guess I'll have to think of something else."

"Your family will be glad to hear it. I don't imagine they were too thrilled with the idea of you going into something as dangerous as police work."

"Oh, they didn't know," she murmured, eyeing George's earlobe with sudden speculation. Career counseling be damned, what would he do if she—

"You didn't tell them? I thought families told each other everything."

She tore her gaze away from his ear. Unfortunately for her attention span, it landed on his mouth. "Not all families. Mine doesn't really understand me that well. They love me, but I never did fit in."

Silence. Then: "Candy?"

"Hmm?"

His fingers tensed on her hip. "Did you mean it?"

Still contemplating his mouth, she nodded absently. "Sure. I don't fit in."

"No, I—what you said before. Did you mean it?"

The sudden intensity in his voice drew her eyes up to meet his. As soon as they locked stares she knew he wasn't talking about her family. "I meant it."

His searching gaze ran over her face. "I don't see how—"

Her heart swelled with tenderness as she laid two fingers across his mouth. "Then let me show you," she whispered, and replaced her fingers with her lips. She let the kiss deepen slowly, probing delicately with her tongue. As his arms looped around her waist she slid over him and trailed kisses across his cheek.

"I love you," she murmured against his ear. Smiling at his indrawn breath, she gently closed her teeth on his earlobe.

"Oh, honey."

His hands coasted up her back, his fingers tangled lightly in her hair. She let him pull her back to his mouth, pressing her fingertips against the back of his neck as she sank into the kiss. When her mind started to blur she pulled away and slid down his body.

"I love you," she repeated against the underside of his jaw. Her tongue lapped at the pulse hammering in his throat, swirled around his nipples, dipped into his navel. His long, strong body heated and tensed, quivering like a drawn bow. She felt her own body respond, her blood heat as she continued downward.

He clasped her shoulders. "Sweetheart, you don't have to—"

"I love you," she said a third time, and lost herself in the pleasure of giving him pleasure, loving him with hands, lips, and tongue until he grabbed her by the shoulders and hauled her up his body and into a fierce kiss.

She didn't know when turnabout happened, but all of a sudden George's hands and mouth were streaking over her as sensation raced through her in stunning waves.

It was agony.

It was ecstasy.

It was incitement to riot.

Her breathless pleas streamed together into a long, gratified groan when he finally sank into her. Then his lips crushed hers, and they both lost control.

His thrusts were forceful, but so were hers. He held her tightly, kissed her voraciously. Her clasp was just as tenacious, her mouth as feverish as his. Perfectly matched in passion, they didn't bother to scale the peak.

They simply threw themselves off of it.

TWELVE

"This place is a real dive, isn't it?" Candy was obviously delighted. "I've never been in a biker bar before."

Price scowled down at her gilt head. "You shouldn't be in one now, dammit," he muttered, sliding into the booth to sit next to her.

The booth was the same one he and Geb had used a couple of nights ago. The music had been turned down, but the raw-meat crowd was just as grungy, the table even filthier than it had been. Candy didn't seem to notice. She swept an enthusiastic gaze around Hog Heaven, looking for all the world like a kid in a toy store.

"I told you I wasn't letting you out of my sight," she reminded him.

"So you eavesdropped to find out where I'd be. Nasty habit, babe."

"Unless you're dealing with a slippery, secretive"— she glanced around again then finished smoothly— "gym teacher. In that case, eavesdropping is good strategy. Besides . . ." She turned a limpid look on him. "Can I help it if I happened to pick up the extension while you were talking to Geb?"

He raked a disgruntled glare over her attire. White T-shirt, black leather jacket, and a pair of jeans that fit like a shrunken glove. "No more than you could help it if you *happened* to stow away under the tarp in my Jeep dressed like Hell's Angel Barbie, I guess."

"See there? I knew you'd understand. A woman's got to do what a woman's got to do."

Just what I need, Shane on estrogen. He crooked a finger under her chin, forcing her to meet his gaze. "I have a job to do."

"And I promise not to get in your way."

Said the blonde, blue-eyed bundle of distractions. He sighed. "Sweetheart, you were born to get in a man's way." Releasing her chin, he signaled for service.

"I'm taking that as a compliment," Candy warned him, and turned to the approaching waitress. Her gaze latched on to the python-wrapped arm, her eyes widened. "Nice tattoo," she said when the woman reached their table.

"Thanks." Clearly pleased to meet a fellow art lover, the waitress from hell extended her arm and twisted her wrist. The snake writhed sinuously. "The guy who did it is real good. I could give you his card if you want."

Candy blinked. "Oh . . . uh, I don't know . . . I mean, it's a beautiful snake, but I don't think . . . I'm not really into reptiles."

"No problem. Vinnie can do any kind of animal you want. Tarantulas, bats, you name it."

Another blink. "Really? Tarantulas?"

"Yeah. He did one for my boyfriend . . . Bobby? A big, hairy sucker right on his—"

"Beer," Price interjected firmly. "Two bottles."

Candy turned to him, eyes dancing with mischief, and whined, "But, honey, I want to hear about Bobby's big, hairy tarantula."

"You'd love it," Snake Woman assured her. "It's right on his—"

"Make it three beers," Price snapped, and glowered over the waitress's shoulder at Geb. "You just going to stand there all night grinning like an idiot?"

"Nope." Geb stepped around the waitress and sat on the opposite bench. "I want to hear about Bobby's spider too."

Candy welcomed Geb with a conspirator's wink. "Not just any spider, a—"

"Tarantula," said Snake Woman. "Right on his—"

"Get the damned beer," growled Price.

"—shoulder," finished the waitress at the same time, and glared at him. "What the *hell* is your problem, pal?"

Lips twitching, Geb asked, "Yeah, what is your problem, bro?"

"He's got this thing about spiders." Candy gave Price's arm a solicitous pat that had him grinding his teeth. "It's, like, a phobia, you know?" She sounded about three IQ points dumber than dirt.

"Oh." The waitress gave Candy a commiserating glance. "That's too bad. A tarantula would've looked good on you. Well, I'll get your beers."

Ignoring Gebhardt's chuckle, Price narrowed his

eyes at Candy. "Having fun?" he asked with lethal softness.

She smiled sweetly, patted his cheek. "You bet. Now introduce me to your partner."

The woman just didn't have the sense to be intimidated. Price washed a hand down his face and gave in. "Jamal Gebhardt, meet Candy Johnson, a.k.a. Trouble."

Candy shook her head and offered a hand across the table. "You'll have to excuse George. He's sulking again."

"Sulking?" Geb's lean, dark fingers wrapped around her pale hand. He was having the time of his life and it showed. "How come?"

"Never mind." Price leveled a stare intended to remind his partner exactly with whom his loyalty lay. He wasn't surprised when Geb answered with a wide, gleeful grin.

Candy shrugged. "He didn't want to bring me along—"

"Damn right," gritted Price.

"—but I hid in his Jeep and came anyway," she finished smugly. "He really hates it when I get the drop on him."

"You did not get the drop on me."

"Sure I did. I'm here, aren't I?"

Geb snorted. "She's got you there, man." He grinned at Candy. "Did you bring the frying pan?"

Candy's head whipped toward Price, her eyes sizzling with outrage. "You *told* him?"

"He's my partner. Of course I told him I broke cover . . . and why."

She threw up her hands in disgust. "Great. Now he'll never like me."

"Yes, I will," said Geb. The traitor.

Candy beamed. "You will?"

"Sure. I've wanted to dust him off a time or two myself."

"I think," Price interrupted grimly, "we should get down to business here." He turned a baleful eye on his partner. "You did pay a visit to the Farmers today?"

After an assessing glance at Candy, Geb shrugged and leaned back in his seat. "Yeah, Traynor and I gave them the full G-man treatment. Dark suits, terse questions, and penetrating looks. The whole bit."

"And?"

"They ate it up. The old lady wanted to touch my badge."

"Terrific." Price swore and raked his fingers through his hair. "Did you get anything besides an inflated ego and a shield full of smudged partials?"

"Show some respect. You're talking to one of America's unsung heroes here. Just ask Ethel May." Geb smirked, and slipped a small spiral notebook out of his pocket. Flipping it open, he read, "Farmer, Duff, age sixty-seven. Married forty-seven years to Ethel May, *née* Winston, age sixty-five. No children. He's a former salesman who specialized in used cars, job hopping, and long periods on unemployment due to unspecified 'health problems.'"

"Mostly a severe allergic reaction to work of any kind," said Candy.

Geb nodded. "That was my take."

The waitress materialized out of the murk and

plunked three bottles on the table. "Big guy like you afraid of spiders," she said with a pitying look at Price, shook her head, and left. He aimed a gimlet stare at Candy.

Geb cleared his throat. "Five years ago Duff got lucky in a private and totally illegal poker game, winning ten acres of nothing just outside of Donnerton. He hopped the Social Security gravy train, got him and Ethel May a thirty-foot trailer and a lot to park it on." He looked up from his notes. "Now pay attention, children, because this is where the story gets real interesting. A couple of years later he bought the missus a PC. . . ."

"So that's how they got tangled up with Grass Roots," Candy mused. "Via the Net."

Gebhardt peered at her, his expression that of a dark, very menacing scientist examining a new species of microbe. "How'd you guess?"

"No guess to it. Ethel May is the Big Kahuna Mama of Net surfers. She's the only one in Donnerton with a Web page."

Geb nodded slowly. "Right. And two and a half years ago she point-and-clicked her way onto Easy Street by way of the Cash for Crops Web site. Cyber digs of"—he sketched quotes in the air—"an agricultural conglomerate that leases land, plants, and harvests the ever-popular, but unspecified 'cash crop,' and gives the lessor a nice cut of the profits."

George grunted. "Labor-free income. Right up old

Duff's alley. You think the Farmers knew the score before you and Traynor showed up on their doorstep?"

Gebhardt shook his head. "The score? Listen, unless that old man's the deffest con artist walking, they didn't even know there was a game on."

"Duff's a terrible liar," Candy said, and watched two pairs of eyes go flat and deadly. The transformation was impressive but uncalled for. "No, no. I mean he's no good at it. He scratches his forearm and his upper lip sweats."

"You," said Geb slowly, "are one scary woman." His gaze shifted to George. "A *very* scary woman. We could have used her when we interrogated Joey Carter last month."

"I told you she was a natural," George pointed out complacently, proving once and for all that there was nothing like an *I told you so* to soothe a wounded male ego.

"If Duff passed the scratch-and-sweat test, you can be sure he's telling the truth." Candy glanced at George. "You were right, he hasn't looked past the corn. Actually, given the figure on the check stub you found, I'd say he hasn't looked past the nose on his face. Only a dunce would believe there was that kind of money in vegetables."

"Not necessarily. Maybe Duff's the gullible type," suggested George.

"Oh, he had the big-money answers," said Geb. "See, that's not just any old corn growing out on his patch of boondocks, that's gen-u-ine, dee-luxe, gourmette popcorn. Real exotic stuff. Imported from Paris. France."

"Poor Duff." Candy sighed. "He might be a lazy, gullible dunce, but he's basically honest. There must have been quite an explosion when you told them the truth."

"Uh-huh." Geb grinned at George. "I haven't heard so many four-letter words since the last time you and the boss butted heads. That Ethel May sure does have some mouth on her."

Candy gaped. "Four-letter . . . *Ethel May?*"

"None other. Seems Miz Farmer had big plans for this year's cut. Wanted to redo the family room. It's kind of hard to be sure, what with all the screaming and cussing, but I think we got the decorating scheme, in detail, right down to the plush red carpet under the twin BarcaLoungers she was gonna buy."

It was all too easy to imagine how plush red carpet would impact the Farmers' decor. Candy winced. "Well, the Farmers might not thank you guys for throwing a monkey wrench into their redecorating plans, but I for one am deeply grateful."

Amused understanding lit George's eyes as he reached up to tug her hair before settling an arm across her shoulders to pull her close. "That's why they call us public servants, baby. Besides, we're not interested in their thanks. We want their cooperation, and if my partner over there did his job right, we'll get it."

She glanced at Gebhardt, who seemed both fascinated and amused at the byplay. "Will they cooperate?"

"It was touch-and-go until Traynor promised Ethel May she'd get her BarcaLoungers. I sure as hell wouldn't want to be in that man's shoes if the paperwork doesn't go through."

"It'll go through," muttered George. It was the *or else* in his voice that had Candy studying him covertly as he and his partner talked.

This tall, dark package of subtly leashed power had been lurking behind the dweeb of her dreams. Hard to believe was an understatement. In retrospect she couldn't understand how he'd put it over on her, because looking at him now made it next to impossible to picture him as anything *Webster's* would define as nerdish. Looking at him now brought a whole new set of adjectives to mind: tough, smart, and untamed among them. Not to mention drop-dead handsome.

Maybe the clothes didn't make the man, she reflected wryly, but they could certainly camouflage him. More than a month ago she'd taken one look at Donnerton's newest faculty member and thought, *If it looks like a greasy goofball and acts like a greasy goofball . . .*

Well, the rest was history.

Her glance ran over him again, taking in the black mane that waved to his collar, the piercing gray gaze, the chiseled lips, and square jaw. He was a sterling specimen of pure male and all muscle in a navy pullover and faded jeans. If this was a greasy goofball, she was Tommy LaSorda.

The surface changes were remarkable, but the real transformation ran much deeper and was twice as stunning.

His so-called undercurrents were broadcasting loud and clear and on all frequencies. This man played deep, and he played to win. He'd seen too much to believe he could save the world, but that didn't stop him from battling to rescue the occasional corner. He was strong, sharp, and tenacious. Potentially lethal. And when push came to shove, he wouldn't give an inch he didn't think he could wrest back later.

Candy let her gaze trail around the room, feeling a sisterly sympathy for Lois Lane. When a woman went to bed with a dork in glasses, the last thing she expected to wake up to was the Man of Steel. Her rueful smile slid absently over a mountain of leather, chains, and hair sitting two tables away. She glanced back at George, missing the biker's answering grin, gap-toothed and delighted.

"How can they be sure that's when it's going down?" George asked. He practically vibrated with excitement, and Candy was chagrined to realize she'd missed something important.

"When what goes down?" she wanted to know. Of course, men on a mission being men on a mission, they ignored the "helpless" woman in their midst.

"Evidently old Duff almost blew a couple of them away with his shotgun the first time they showed up," Geb chortled. "Guess he thought they were popcorn poachers or something. Now they make damned sure he knows when they're coming."

"Duff almost shot somebody?" She didn't get an answer to that one either.

She *did* get an affectionate, if condescending, glance from George. "Drink your beer, honey. We're almost through here." He looked back at Gebhardt. "Okay, set it up."

Things were starting to gel. Candy looked from

one man to the other. "Set it up. You mean the ambush. You know exactly when the Grass Roots people are coming, thanks to Duff's itchy trigger finger." Her eyes narrowed on George's face. "When?"

"You don't need to know," he said. She stared at him then eyed her beer, but he snatched the bottle out of reach before she could dump it all over his beautiful, chauvinistic head. "It's government business, baby."

"But—"

He whipped out a coaxing version of The Smile and the objection stalled on her lips, giving him time to reach up and cup her cheek. "Please, sweetheart, stay out of it. You're a civilian and you could get hurt." His eyes turned hard as The Smile disappeared. "Then I'd probably have to kill somebody," he muttered.

She couldn't block the sigh of the lovesick sap. He hadn't said he loved her, but a steely look of concern-cum-death-threat was definitely progress. "Forget I asked."

No concession at all, since she was determined to find out everything she needed to know on her own.

"Thanks." He dropped a light kiss on her lips. If she hadn't been convinced that she'd be snooping for his own good, Candy might have felt guilty. As it was, she heaved a dispirited sigh and glanced away.

The knot in her stomach eased when she heard about the number of DEA agents that would be involved. It eased more during the reassuring discussion about choppers and long-range weapons. The operation was as well planned and precisely timed as a military campaign, and they didn't even expect their visitors to be armed. Thoughts she'd studiously avoided—like the ones where George got hurt or, God forbid, killed—faded into the realm of the highly unlikely.

Relief washed through her, softening her eyes as they roamed aimlessly around the bar. No doubt the whole thing would be over before she knew it, and she and George would be back in bed making celebratory love. The thought brought a wide smile of anticipation to her face. The smile died a quick death when the beefy biker she hadn't known she was looking at nodded, climbed to his feet, and hitched up his leather pants.

Uh-oh.

He lumbered toward them.

Damn. She gave a tense pat to the hand resting on her right shoulder. "George?"

He captured her fingers, giving them an absent squeeze. "Be with you in a second, honey," he said. "We've got a couple important details to work out."

Candy glanced at the behemoth bearing down on their table. Did something that weighed close to two-fifty and looked like an amorous grizzly on a bad hair day qualify as an important detail? She had a strong, unpleasant hunch they were about to find out.

"Hairy" was almost on them. Candy stiffened, her trapped fingers fluttered frantically in George's grip. "Heads up, guys, I think we've got—"

"You ready to split this joint, sweet mama?" The biker's voice was a slow growl-drawl reminiscent of John Wayne on steroids and downers.

Geb went still. George went still. All of Hog

Heaven went still as George's head turned, very slowly. "Get lost, pal. The lady is with me."

It was as if he hadn't spoken. The grizzly's beady black eyes never left Candy's face. "I got my hog gassed up and ready to go." A huge, grubby paw reached across George to latch onto her arm. "So let's ride. I wanna be in Bakersfield by sunrise."

She was about to consign him and his sunrise to a place even hotter than Bakersfield when George forcefully removed the paw from her arm and stood. "Didn't quite catch the drift, huh? Let me see if I can make this simple. Like you." He laid a hand on Candy's shoulder. "She's mine."

"Yeah, I'm his," she snapped, and beamed at George when he flashed her an exasperated look. Across the booth Geb coughed into his hand.

Hairy nodded ponderously. "Sure, I know how it is. You're his right now, but you don't wanna be. That's why you smiled at me. You know Bear can take care of you."

George's head swung around. "You made eye contact with a guy named Bear in a biker bar? You smiled at him?"

"I didn't know his name was Bear, and I didn't smile *at* him," Candy muttered, "I smiled *toward* him. There's a difference. I was thinking about how after everything was over you and I would—" She sputtered to a belated halt, miserably certain that her fiery cheeks glowed brighter than the neon-lit jukebox.

"Oh, we will, sweetheart," he drawled quietly. Geb chuckled and cleared his throat as George turned back to Bear. "You've made a mistake. The lady is happy where she is."

"Too bad. I want her, and I'm gonna take her." Bear made to step around his shorter, slighter opponent and found himself blocked.

"Over my dead body, you bastard," snarled George quietly.

Bear shrugged. "Okay," he said, and lunged.

"You should have let me hit him."

Price felt his lips twitch as he glanced across the Jeep. Candy's sulky pout was bathed in the glow of the dashboard lights. "Honey, he was already on his way down. Even if you'd managed to connect with that beer bottle, he wouldn't have felt a thing."

"Maybe not, but *I* would have. I can't believe that cretin had the nerve to try to kick you in your . . . You should have let me hit him," she growled.

"I let you trip the waitress."

"Hah! Geb didn't even feel it when she whacked him with that tray. She's got a pathetic forehand, all snake and no muscle. I know out of shape when I sit on it." A second later he heard her mutter, "Just one good hit."

He remembered the fierce outrage on her face when Bear had tried to drop-kick him into eunuchhood, and grinned. One good hit, hell, she would have killed the guy. "I'm sorry, baby. Want to go back and finish him off?"

"Don't give me that. You know the police probably took everybody away. Getting us out of there was smart thinking," she conceded grudgingly. "Even if you did throw me over your shoulder to do it."

"Hey, I tried to reason with you, but you had blood in your eye, a bottle in your hand, and Bear in your sights. Over the shoulder was my only option."

"Maybe." She paused, probably nibbled on her lip. Then in a rush: "You think Geb's all right?"

"Better than all right. Nothing he loves more than a good brawl. Has ever since he was a skinny kid with more guts than sense."

"You've known him since you were kids?"

"Yeah. His mom used to say we were closer than Siamese twins joined at the hip. She had the postfight routine down pat. We'd get Bactine, bandages, and a lecture, win or lose. Then she'd grab her strap and go after the bad guys."

Remembering, he grinned. Mamie Gebhardt, plump dynamo of the sparkling brown eyes and generous smile, had been hell on wheels when it came to protecting her own. And to Mamie's mind, her own included one love-starved white boy.

"So Mrs. Gebhardt and I have something in common." Candy gave the trusty beer bottle tucked in the crook of her right arm an affectionate pat.

"A thirst for bloody justice?"

"Absolutely."

He shook his head, smiling ruefully. "You and Mamie. Kind of makes me feel sorry for the bad guys."

"Well, don't. The bad guys deserve everything they get." Candy paused before saying, oh so casually, "And speaking of bad guys . . . Let's talk about the ambush."

Well, hell, he'd walked right into that one. Price tried a sidestep into semantics. "Stakeout. Bad-guys ambush, the forces-of-law-and-order stakeout."

"Okay, let's talk about the stakeout."

"What's to talk about? You heard the plan, you know how the bust will go down."

"But I don't know *when* the bust will go down."

"And you agreed to let it go."

Out of the corner of his eye he saw her shift in her seat. "Not exactly. I told you to forget I asked." Her chin lifted. "Well, forget I told you to forget. I want to know."

Price thought about telling her. Why not? She was smart, and she wouldn't talk. So what could it hurt?

Common sense thundered to his rescue. This was the woman who'd followed a suspicious character to a deserted house, stowed away on a meet between two federal agents, and waded with gusto into a brawl in a biker bar. The question wasn't *what* could telling her hurt, but *who?* The answer chilled him right down to the bone.

He heard the tap of a booted foot on the floorboard. "Well?"

"I'm thinking."

"Thinking. Listen, George, it's simple. Either you tell me or I find out on my own."

She'd do it too. It would be easy. All she had to do was have a woman-to-woman chat with Ethel May, and she'd know just enough to get in harm's way. The hair on the back of his neck lifted. How did a man keep his woman safe from herself?

Easy. He lied through his teeth. "Tuesday night."

The bust was actually going down late Monday night, but he was confident he'd be able to sneak out, take care of business, and be back in bed with her before dawn. At which time he'd drain off the head of steam she'd build up when she found out he lied to her in the first place by making love with her again.

This was not only a plan, it was a plan with perks. *Oh, the sacrifices a man makes for duty, honor, and country,* he thought, and grinned.

"Why are you smiling like that?" He met Candy's suspicious gaze. "You're telling me the truth, aren't you?"

His conscience didn't even flinch. He pulled into her driveway, cut the engine, and looked her right in the eye. "Tuesday night, I swear."

Her narrowed eyes probed his face which he kept carefully shuttered. Finally, she nodded. "Okay." And yawned.

His shoulders relaxed as he smiled. "Come on, honey, let's get you to bed. You've had a busy night." He hustled her into the house, convinced that potential disaster had been averted.

Of course he should have known it wouldn't be that easy.

THIRTEEN

Like ivy on a wall, she was all over him. Candy slept with one long leg thrown on top of Price's thighs, her left arm stretched across his chest, her hand cupping his shoulder. Her right hand wrapped his biceps, and her face was tucked against his neck.

He gave himself a minute to ponder the questionable sanity of leaving a warm tangle of naked woman to squat in a frosty cornfield. With a regretful sigh, he carefully peeled away the temptation to stay right where he was. It was almost eleven, and he had to go.

Ten minutes later he stood in front of the full-length mirror, a tall, powerful silhouette dressed in clothes as black as the paint he methodically smeared on his face.

His glance flicked to the windows reflected behind him. The moonless night was tailor-made for a stakeout . . . or for eluding one. Win, lose, or draw was a matter of timing and luck now, and like any good cop, Price had a healthy respect for the capriciousness of both. The best-laid plan could go lethally astray in the blink of an eye.

He stepped back to critique his appearance. A sinister figure swathed in shadow stared back at him. His lips thinned grimly as it occurred to him that he spent entirely too much time in shadow. He turned, his pensive gaze falling on the bright head resting on his erstwhile pillow. Was she his last chance to step into the light?

He moved to the bed and stared down at Candy, a wry smile twisting his lips. It wouldn't take her long to add together two and two and come up with the fact that he'd plied her with wine and lovemaking in order to put her out of commission.

Come the dawn, there will definitely be hell to pay, he thought, and the smile widened.

So be it. He'd pay hell with interest, he admitted as the smile faded, if it meant keeping her safe. He had to keep her safe. Because he knew with sudden blinding certainty that he couldn't live without her.

Oh, God. I love her.

The realization slammed into him, knocking him for a loop, rocking him back on his heels. He shook his head as if to clear it, but the truth wouldn't shake loose.

I love her.

Of course you love her, he thought with a silent snort, *a moron could see that.*

Trouble was a smart moron would have picked a better time to grasp the obvious. He had a job to do tonight. He needed to be alert, concentrate. Simultaneous surges of joy and terror weren't conducive to concentration. An alert man didn't stare off into space wondering if he had anything to offer a certain remark-able woman.

Jamming his hands on his hips, Price tipped back his head. He wanted to laugh. He wanted to swear. But more than anything, he wanted to climb back in that bed and make love with his woman until she knew he loved her and they both got used to the idea.

That's just what he'd do, he promised himself on a step forward, then stopped. This time he did swear. Because getting used to the idea would have to wait until first thing in the morning.

She was thirsty and cold, and something was miss-ing. No, not something. Candy's hand swept the bed, searching blindly. Some*one*. "George?"

Her eyes opened on a wide yawn that melted into a pout when she found out she had the bed to herself. According to her alarm clock, it was almost midnight. Too late to sleep alone.

Shoving aside the covers, she got up and padded to the bathroom, flipped on the light, and scowled at the sleep-tousled woman in the mirror. "Well, where is he?" The woman stared back at her, equally disgrun-tled and just as clueless. "Big help you are," Candy muttered, and stumbled back into the hallway. "George?"

Columbo, a cat of great tact and sensitivity who slept on the sofa these days, opened his eyes and re-garded her quizzically. She scowled down at him. "Do you know where he is?"

Five minutes later she definitely knew where

George wasn't. He wasn't at her place, and his Jeep wasn't in her driveway. Heart pounding, nerves crawling with dread, she sank onto the sofa, absently stroking Columbo when he leaped into her lap.

"He could have gone out for pizza. Or home to pick up something. Clean socks maybe." Stupid explanations. Sure they were stupid. But she'd take idiotic theory any day over what she suddenly knew to be fact.

He wouldn't. As a cold sweat broke out on her forehead, she reviewed all the good, sensible reasons why the man she loved would *not* go out to the Farmer property alone.

The stakeout was scheduled for tomorrow night. An army of agents would be there. Tomorrow night. Helicopters and long-range weapons would be there. Tomorrow night. Heck, even the criminals were on for tomorrow night. So George had no reason to go out to that cornfield tonight.

Unless he wanted to be sure the Grass Roots Gang didn't sneak in ahead of time.

Candy shook her head. George wouldn't do anything stupid like, say, try to close the window of opportunity without backup. An experienced agent knew better, and he was an experienced agent.

Who felt handcuffed by the system, she remembered with fresh alarm. Who'd committed a felony without batting an eye to prod the case along. Who'd been very free with the wine and lovemaking a few hours earlier in what now looked like a blatant attempt to anesthetize her so he could sneak off.

But he wouldn't go out to that remote cornfield at midnight without backup.

"Says who?" Candy surged to her feet and dumped an indignant Columbo onto the sofa. Terror chased her into the bedroom and fueled a rush of adrenaline that had her yanking open a drawer with enough force to tear it out of the dresser.

"And to think I stopped calling him Pinhead. Damn menace," she muttered, jerking a pair of gray sweats from the jumble on the floor.

She was barely put together when she streaked out the front door less than five minutes later. Incidentals like socks and underwear had been lost in the rush. She did remember to jam her feet into a pair of running shoes, but failed to notice they were unlaced until she dashed out of them on her way to the car.

Pedal to the metal wasn't meant for backing up, but Candy floored it, and the Honda shot out of the driveway like an arrow in reverse. It hadn't come to a complete stop before she slammed it into first and laid a strip of rubber big enough to patch the Goodyear blimp.

Reinforcements, she thought frantically as the car rocketed down the road. She had to get reinforcements. Except she didn't know Geb's phone number or who else to call. That left local talent, she concluded, and groaned.

A desperate glance at her dashboard clock showed quarter after twelve, and she swore ripely. How in the hell was she supposed to find reinforcements after midnight in a town where every able-bodied citizen went to bed at dusk? She'd have to make do with the less than able-bodied, and all of a sudden she knew exactly where to find them.

"Yes!" The flat of her hand slapped triumphantly against the steering wheel, the car swerved dangerously, Candy yelped. She clamped both hands on the wheel, corrected her trajectory, and took a steadying breath. "Straighten up and drive right, Johnson. You've got cavalry to round up."

"Will you knock it off?" Price murmured. Geb had been humming almost soundlessly for the last twenty minutes. "One more chorus of 'Proud Mary' and I'm going to—"

Geb's whisper frosted the air between them. "Hey, man, I'm just getting into the mood here. It's my turn on the flamethrower."

Price rolled a look heavenward. *I am crouched in a damned cornfield. I am freezing my butt off. I've got a cramp in my left leg and a pyromaniac for a partner. Meanwhile the beautiful woman who loves me is sleeping alone. Does this make any kind of sense?*

It was a rhetorical question, and the obvious answer was rendered moot by a muted click from his headset. Tedium and physical discomfort were immediately forgotten. Price felt his senses sharpen to razor alertness even before he heard the transmission. "They're on their way."

Automatically checking his position and equipment, he reviewed the plan. The men and women strung around the field's perimeter would move in and spring the trap as soon as their visitors picked enough hemp to hang themselves. His lips thinned in grim satisfac-

tion. Barring any unforeseen circumstances, this bust
would be a cakewalk.

And it should have been a cakewalk. Except unforeseen circumstances refused to be barred.

The NRA had a lot going for it, Candy decided as
she sprinted across the parking lot. Guns and plenty of
them. At least half of those guns seemed to be promi-
nently displayed in window racks in the muscular pickups strewn around her. The patrons of the Happy
Camper Grill obviously had a penchant for horsepower
with firepower.

Good. Speed was of the essence, and the right to
bear arms was beginning to look like her favorite con-
stitutional amendment.

An eerily glowing porthole punctuated the Happy
Camper's massive door, a slab of oak she all but ripped
off the hinges as she stumbled into the second dive
she'd visited in three days. Thanks to George, she'd be
making quite a name for herself before long. *Just call
me barfly*.

Unlike Hog Heaven, which reminded her of a concrete cave, the Happy Camper sported wooden walls
hung with beer signs, a herd of deer antlers, and a
mounted trout the size of Jaws. The crowd in denim
and baseball caps looked as if they'd tippled through
several consecutive happy hours.

She noticed these things peripherally as she crossed
to the bar. Perched on the nearest stool Henry Mc-

Adam hefted a pilsner glass, working diligently on his beer belly with his eyes glued to the television set mounted in the corner.

Candy clutched his red flannel sleeve. "Henry, I—"

"Bottom of the sixth, two outs," he bellowed. "Dodgers are up by one." And that's when she remembered he was practically deaf.

Desperately aware that time was running out, she whirled to face the man behind her. "Chet, please, I need your help."

"What?" Tall, gangly Chet Lewis swiveled on his bar stool. "What's that?"

"I need your help."

He shook his head and jabbed a finger toward the jukebox. "You gotta speak up." Suddenly he scowled, his fiery brows snapping together. "Hey, what're you doin' here anyway? This isn't any place for a woman."

You're telling me, and I'm getting nowhere fast, she thought with a wild lunge at the jukebox. Nobody minded her mad scrabble for the cord, but when she jerked the plug and snuffed Pam Tillis right in the middle of her "Crazy Life," a few indignant *what the hells* grumbled up.

Candy clambered onto the bar, planting herself between the viewing audience and home plate. "Listen, everybody, I—" Her clarion call to arms was cut short by a drunken hoot from the vicinity of the pool table.

"Well, awww right! We got us one of them exotic dancers! Crank 'er up, honey! Shake that thing!"

Mac the bartender's thunderous glare sliced from Candy to the back of the room. "I told you not to have that last beer, Winston. And you're a damn site drunker than I thought you were if you can't tell the difference between an exotic dancer and a gym teacher."

Beefy Winston Powell squinted through the smoke, leaning heavily on his cue stick. "Gym teacher? Well, hell. What's she doing up there on the bar if she ain't—"

"Will you shut up and listen?" Candy roared, and silence fell like a ton of bricks. She drew a deep breath. "I need a few good men." Winston and his lewd grin stepped forward, so her hand shot up while she clarified. "Actually, I need a posse."

The occasional rustle of corn and the now-you-see-it-now-you-don't wink of a flashlight assured Price that things were going according to plan. Any minute now the radio would click twice, a signal that all good agents should tiptoe through the cornstalks and close the net. Anticipation zinged through his system, the need for caution brushing along behind it. Both were familiar.

The icy trickle of foreboding that slid down his spine in their wake was something new.

He tensed, fighting a bizarre urge to whip out his .45 and . . . Do what, dammit? What the hell was wrong with him? It wasn't the wait, because he'd waited longer and in worse places. Fourteen sweltering hours in an extremely ripe Dumpster, for example.

He couldn't blame his uneasiness on the risk factor either. Okay, any bust could turn sour, but terms like *life threatening* didn't usually apply when a battalion of agents closed in on a bunch of yuppified flower children gone bad like Grass Roots.

So spoke his common sense.

But his instincts were screaming, and he knew better than to ignore them. When the two clicks finally sounded he unholstered his weapon and started to slip silently down the corn row, fully expecting to run into a serious screwup.

The thought flitted through his mind that he could be damned thankful Candy was where she belonged, at home and in the dark.

"Tell them to cut the lights," Candy murmured. Best keep George and . . . whoever in the dark. For now.

"That's a Roger." Chet's voice vibrated with barely suppressed excitement as he reached for the mike on his CB.

Candy winced. Not for the first time since she and her tipsy troops had streamed out of the Happy Camper, she wondered if riding to the rescue was the right thing to do. Her uneasy gaze flicked from Chet on her left to Winston on her right. They looked tense but enthusiastic.

Loose cannons probably always looked tense but enthusiastic.

Let's just forget the whole thing, shall we? She opened her mouth to say it, but the words died with the birth of an image of George bleeding in a cornfield. She shut her mouth and nibbled her lip. If this mission was a mistake, it was a mistake she had to make.

"You'd better stop here," she said when they reached the sweeping curve just ahead of Farmer's field. "There might be somebody watching the road."

"A lookout, you mean. Good thinking." Chet gave her an eager, approving glance that had her wincing again as he pulled over.

A line of pickups slid in behind them. Candy stepped onto the shoulder and watched her Happy Camper militia pile out. Taking a deep breath, she raised a hand and signaled for them to follow.

But she couldn't stem a rising sense of dread.

He couldn't stem the rising sense of dread. There was no shaking it, and he was done trying. This whole gig was about to go way wrong. Price locked gazes with Geb and caught a tight nod that had him reaching for the transmit button on his headset.

The distant hum of motors. A panicked whisper, close by. "Did you hear that? Somebody's coming, dammit. Let's get the hell out of here!" A shouted warning followed by loud thrashing as bodies broke through the corn in headlong flight.

With a soft, vicious curse Price keyed the mike. "They're spooked. Get those damned choppers in here! We need lights—now!"

Two bulky shadows materialized a few yards ahead of him in the darkened row. They stumbled toward him, blind rats in a dark trap until one of them remembered to turn on his flashlight. As bad luck would have it, the halogen beam sliced into Price's eyes, shrinking his pupils to pinpoints.

"DEA," he barked, and dropped to one knee, his weapon gripped in both hands. "Freeze!"

A third body broke through the wall of stalks and crashed into the first two. All three perps tumbled to the ground as Geb ghosted in on their rear. *Snick.* That's all it took. The sound of a safety sliding off behind them stopped any and all attempts to rise.

"On your faces, arms out to your sides," ordered Geb. He kept them covered while Price patted them down. Aside from the small pocketknives they'd been using to cut the buds, they were clean.

A faint *whup-whup* had Price glancing up to see the first chopper rise over the tree line, its floodlight blazing like a miniature sun.

"About time," he muttered, and gestured with his .45. "On your feet, hands behind your head. We're—"

An exultant whoop off to his left had him stiffening as a voice called out, "There's one! Hey, you! Come back here!"

The next voice they heard was Traynor's. "You, with the rifle. Freeze and drop your weapon."

"Rifle?" The prisoner closest to Gebhardt looked from Geb to his accomplices to Price. He shook his shaggy head. "Not one of our guys, man. We are strictly into nonviolence."

"I said drop it!" snapped Traynor.

"Now, you just hold on, mister," growled the first voice. "I don't know who in the *hell* you think you are—"

A familiar, distressed feminine cry froze the blood in Price's veins. "Chet, don't!"

Geb shot him a sharp look. "Wasn't that—"

"Who else? Dammit to hell!" Price was already moving. He'd managed six running steps and a short prayer when the first shot rang out.

FOURTEEN

"Men," Candy muttered, and crossed her arm. The left one. Her right was handcuffed to a chair. "It's not like anybody got hurt," she groused with an irritable glance at George.

Studiously avoiding the bloodthirsty glares of the twenty not-so-Happy Campers sardined in the two cells to her right, Candy let her gaze travel around Donnerton's jail—a short, unpleasant trip that included two cells, an old metal desk, three chairs, a beat-up file cabinet, a closet-sized bathroom, three DEA agents, the sheriff and his deputy, and the Happy Campers.

"Men," she muttered again. "Who needs them? Not me, brother." Especially when the men in question had that lynch-mob look in their eye, and all for her.

She could only be thankful the Grass Roots Gang had been hauled directly to some other jail without passing Go, because they probably wanted her scalp the same as everybody else. You'd think the whole fiasco had been her fault.

Candy grimaced and felt herself blush. Okay, the fiasco part *had* been mostly her fault, because the DEA operation had been going like clockwork until she'd blundered onto the scene with twenty armed drunks. The fact that nobody had been hurt was directly traceable to luck, the dark, and some really lousy shooting.

But, geez, didn't these guys recognize extenuating circumstances when a woman explained them over and over? She was in love, dammit. She'd believed her man was in danger. She'd panicked. Was this so hard to understand? Hell, no. So why didn't they give her a break?

"Rush out with no underwear to save your lover's life and this is the thanks you get." Her right hand lifted, metal rattled. "Handcuffed to an ugly chair, pinched black-and-blue by a cracked leather seat while everybody blames you for everything."

George was the worst offender. The last words *he'd* said to her had been yelled at the top of his lungs over two hours earlier. The air over Duff's cornfield was probably still blue.

"Did you say something, Ms. Johnson?" asked James Thorn, and she reluctantly turned to look at him.

George's supervisor wasn't a big man. In fact, he was just about her height, average looking, with hazel eyes and thin brown hair. It was close to three A.M., but the creases in his slacks remained razor sharp and not a wrinkle marred his white shirt. He had yet to so much as fidget with his tie. His ruthlessly immaculate appearance and her recent period of forced observation led her to believe that he was a stickler for details, rules, and regulations.

The handcuff he'd personally slapped on her wrist led her to believe that her butt was in a sling.

"Ms. Johnson?"

"Will you please take these off?" She tugged on her right hand. "You made your bust and got all the bad guys, I'm not going anywhere, and nobody got hurt. It's not like I'm some dangerous weirdo, you know."

Something between a snarl and a curse rolled out of the chair next to Hiram Walters's desk, because that's where George sat explaining things to the sheriff. Gebhardt, leaning against the wall by the door, snorted. The caged Happy Campers swore loudly, in obvious and rank disbelief.

Candy whipped an offended glare around the room, cowed absolutely no one, and turned it on Thorn. "Well?"

He slipped a hand into the pocket of his gray suit coat and nodded toward the Happy Campers. "You incited these men to riot, Ms. Johnson."

"I did not incite them to riot," she muttered, then squirmed. "Well, not exactly."

"You obstructed justice, thereby aiding and abetting known felons."

"I was only trying to help." Which was exactly what aiding and abetting meant, she realized, and blurted, "George. I was trying to help George."

Thorn didn't show it by so much as a twitch of his thin lips, but she knew she'd amused him. Her temper rose, only to shrivel and die when he continued, "That may be, but you also resisted arrest."

"Arrest?" Candy's eyes widened, because until now she hadn't thought of it that way. Until now it had just been George tossing her over his shoulder again while she wriggled and kicked and hollered at him to put her down. "But—"

"Actually, whether or not you will officially be placed under arrest has yet to be determined. I've decided to leave the question of charges up to the special agent who directed the operation."

Oh, no. He didn't . . . He couldn't possibly mean . . . "And which special agent would that be?" she asked warily.

Thorn looked at George.

Candy looked at George.

George looked at Candy. The blistering fury in his gaze was hot enough to singe her eyebrows, even from across the room.

She swallowed. "Know any good lawyers, Mr. Thorn?"

"You're sure about this, Hunter?"

The man Candy knew as George Price paused, not because he was unsure of his decision, but because someone had used his real name for the first time in months. The fact that his first name had come out of Thorn's mouth only added to his sense of disorientation. Thorn had called him plenty of names during their numerous run-ins, but Hunter hadn't been one of them.

He dragged a weary hand through his hair and glanced around. Except for Thorn, himself, and Candy—who was fighting off sleep in the corner—the jail was deserted. The good old boy vigilantes had been sent home amid much grumbling with Hiram Walters's stern warning to never get involved with another crazy woman. Sheriff Walters and his deputy had taken Geb to breakfast. The nightmare of a night was over, and it was beginning to look like he'd survived.

"Hunter? If you need time to think it over—"

He drew a deep breath. "No, I'm sure. I've thought about resigning for a long time now."

"The agency will be sorry to lose you." Thorn's lips quirked sardonically as he held out a hand. "You and I had our differences on policy and procedure, but you were a damned fine agent. For a renegade," he added. The faint touch of bitterness put them back on familiar ground and had Hunter grinning.

"Thanks." The handshake was quick, pure formality, and Thorn looked relieved when it was out of the way.

He cleared his throat, shifted uncomfortably. "So, have you made any plans?"

It was one of those pro forma, chitchat questions, but Hunter answered. "Yeah. I thought I'd go private, set up my own agency."

His gaze was drawn back to Candy. She was pale and disheveled, her hair sticking up in little blonde tufts. From the way her head rested against the wall, he knew she'd finally fallen asleep.

"Well, I can't say I'm surprised. You always did like to make your own rules. I take it those plans include

Ms. Johnson?" Still studying Candy's face, Hunter nodded absently. "I always knew you had more guts than were good for you, Hunter, but I never guessed they ran to nerves of steel."

The twist of humor in Thorn's voice caught Hunter's attention. He glanced at the older man, eyebrows raised. "Meaning?"

Thorn turned a wry gaze on Candy. "Meaning I know a handful when I see one. Smart, headstrong, and rash. She suits you."

"I know."

"She'll run you ragged," Thorn said, and there was a good deal of relish in the statement. "I wonder how many nights like this one you're in for."

The memory of Candy's cry punctuated by gunshots had Hunter's blood running cold all over again. He could have lost her, he thought, and shuddered. "There won't *be* any more nights like this one," he vowed grimly. "I'll make damned sure of it."

"If you say so." Thorn sounded both amused and skeptical.

Given Candy's taste for adventure, keeping her out of trouble would be a lifetime Mission Impossible. Hunter sighed philosophically. "Well, hell. I can always resort to handcuffs again. Too bad I didn't think of them before; I could have saved us all a lot of trouble."

"I've lost hair over your antics, Hunter. Pulled it out by the handful. But I have a feeling Ms. Johnson will spend the rest of her life giving you plenty of your own medicine." Thorn sighed beatifically. "Tonight may have spelled trouble for you, but for me it was nothing short of sheer poetic justice."

It was a good dig, but Hunter knew the last trick would be his. And considering all the crap he'd put up with from Thorn over the last couple of years, he would thoroughly enjoy turning that trick.

"Poetic justice?" he asked.

"And nothing but."

"You feel pretty good about that, do you?" Thorn nodded, still smiling widely. "Gives you a lot of satisfaction, huh?"

"You have no idea."

"You might want to savor that feeling for a while. . . ." Hunter paused. "Before you talk to Gebhardt."

The smug smile vanished. "Special Agent Gebhardt has already given me his report."

"Well see, that's just it. He isn't . . . a special agent, that is. Not anymore." Grinning wickedly, he clapped Thorn on the shoulder and started toward Candy.

"What do you mean, he isn't a—" Thorn sputtered before his voice rose in outrage. "Are you telling me Gebhardt is resigning too?"

"Yep." Ignoring the impressive rain of curses behind him, Hunter squatted next to Candy and cupped her cheek. "Hey, sleepyhead, you ready to go home?"

Her eyelids fluttered up. "George?"

"Close enough for government work, honey." He slipped the key out of his pocket, unlocked the cuffs, and scooped her out of the chair.

Her arms wound around his neck, her head

dropped against his shoulder. "You're going to pay for tonight, George," she murmured drowsily. "Big time."

"I know, baby. For the rest of my life." He was looking forward to it.

"Hold it right there, dammit." Thorn planted himself between Hunter and the door. "This is all a plot to get back at me, isn't it? I want you to look me right in the eye and tell me you didn't talk Gebhardt into leaving with you."

Hunter didn't stop, forcing Thorn to either step aside or be run down. "Nah. Getting back at you is just a bonus. Leaving was Geb's idea, he talked me into it. Why don't you go next door to the coffee shop and ask him."

Candy stirred. "You're leaving?"

"Not yet."

And when I do, you're going with me. But he wanted privacy for that discussion, because if she started with *no* he planned to love her into *yes*. For now, he brushed a kiss across her forehead as he settled her in the seat of his Jeep.

"Come back here, you—" Silhouetted in the door of the tiny jailhouse, Thorn shook his fist then stalked over to the Sunnyside Up, open since the crack of dawn an hour earlier. He threw open the door. The little welcome bell tinkled crazily as he thundered, "Gebhardt, I want to talk to you!"

Hunter chuckled, patted Candy's thigh, and put the Jeep in gear.

❖————————❖

"Yes! Oh, George, yes! *Yes!*"

The climax crashed through her in huge, glittering waves that tossed her higher than she'd ever gone before. Arms and legs wrapped around George, Candy held on, lifting her hips into his final deep thrust, her own cry joining his shout of satisfaction as a second release exploded in on the last echoes of her first.

He sank on top of her, his welcome weight pressing her into the mattress. The light rasp of uneven breath was the only sound in the room, and his feathered warmly against her neck as his heartbeat slowed against her breast. The morning sun spilled over his shoulder and into her eyes, its warm golden glow announcing a brand-new day.

Thank God.

The previous night had been longer than the Boston Marathon and twice as grueling. Candy was a physical and emotional basket case. Wrung out would be an improvement. An hour ago she'd been ready to go Sleeping Beauty a year or two better, but then her own personal Prince Charming had kissed her and all of a sudden sleep was the farthest thing from her mind.

Now she was back to exhausted, but she couldn't stop running her hands over his back or dropping the occasional kiss on his shoulder.

She didn't remember much about the last few hours at the jail, having whiled them away in a sleepy fog, but she seemed to remember talk about George leaving. Well, possession was nine tenths of the law, and right now he was with her. Safe and sound. Closing her eyes, she sent up a silent thank-you.

He shifted. His lips touched her ear. "I love you," he whispered.

It was absolutely the last straw. Her emotions had run the gamut, racing from frantic to terrified to slack relief. She'd been shot at, yelled at, threatened with prosecution, and handcuffed to a chair. Finding out that George loved her was just too damned much.

She burst into tears.

"Candy?" He rolled off of her, raised up on one elbow, and touched a finger to her tear-streaked face. "Honey? What is it? What's wrong?"

"Y-you said you love me," she bawled, and socked him.

He gave an obliging "ooof" and rubbed his stomach, but she knew she hadn't really hurt him, because he chuckled warmly and pulled her close, trapping her arms between them. "Well, that explains everything. Hit me again, honey, I deserve it."

"Y-you do not," she wailed. "Oh God, don't look at me. I'm a mess!"

"All right." He tucked her face under his chin. "I won't look." He didn't say anything for a long time, but held her, gently stroking her hair while she blubbered like a baby all over his chest.

"Feel better?" he asked a while later. The flood of tears had ebbed to the occasional watery hiccup, and she nodded. "Are you going to cry every time I tell you I love you?"

"I hope not," she mumbled. As outbursts went, that one had been mortifying. She avoided his gaze as she sat up to pluck a tissue from the box on the nightstand. "I hate to cry. Makes my head feel like it's full of wet cotton, and my eyes—" She broke off as his words finally registered.

Are you going to cry every time I tell you I love you? Her hand froze just short of her soggy, swollen eyes. Her heart picked up a beat as she slowly lowered her hand and turned to look at him.

"Are you—" She swallowed. "Are you planning to say it often?"

His smile, so warm and tender, made her eyes sting all over again. "Only several times a day for the next fifty or sixty years. You're going to rust," he warned as fresh tears welled, and handed her another tissue.

Blinking rapidly, because another bout would probably drown them both, she gave him a damp, but brilliant smile. "I'm going to be around for the next fifty or sixty years?"

"Well, that depends on how you answer my question." He pulled her down next to him and laid a hand on her cheek. His loving, somber gaze sent her heart rocketing into her throat, where it hung and trembled.

"Question?" she squeaked.

"Candy Johnson, you are the smartest, gutsiest, sexiest, most *exasperating* woman alive. You've pulled one harebrained stunt after another since I met you, but nothing to top last night." His voice roughened. "You could have been killed, dammit. Do you have any idea what losing you would have done to me?"

"The same thing that losing you would have done to me, which is why I did what I did. Was that the question?" she asked quickly, because he was about to disagree and she didn't want him to get sidetracked into a lecture. Not if this discussion was headed where she thought it was headed.

"No, that was the setup. And this is the warning: The next time you go off half-cocked, I will personally handcuff you to my bed and throw away the key. *Now* comes the question. Knowing the terms"—his voice deepened and softened—". . . and knowing that I love you more than my life, will you marry me?"

"Yes. Oh, yes!" she cried, and tossed her arms around his neck. "I love you, George."

His arms came around her waist even as he said, "No, you don't."

"Of course I do," she murmured, peppering feverish kisses over his face. "Don't be silly."

"No," he said, with a nip to her chin, "I mean you don't love me, *George*. You love me, Hunter."

"Hunter?" She pulled back to beam at him. "That's your real name?" He nodded. "Hunter." She sighed and kissed him hard, because Hunter sounded so much more dangerous, intriguing, and exciting than George.

One kiss led to another, which led to a caress, which led to . . . well, fifteen minutes later she was on top of him and he was inside her and they were making love again.

"I don't think we can do this every day for fifty or sixty years," she mumbled afterward. She lay sprawled on top of him. "I'm all limp."

His hand drifted lazily down her spine. "So what's wrong with limp? I like you limp."

Candy sighed with satisfaction. "Me too. But there isn't much call for limp gym teachers."

"Mmm-hmm. But then you're not going to be a

gym teacher, which is good, because I plan to make you limp on a regular basis."

"You do? I'm not?" She raised her head to look down at him. "What am I going to be?"

"Exactly what you said you wanted to be."

"Hunter, I can't be a cop now. I explained all that the other night. Red tape and bureaucrats, remember? Don't forget," she muttered darkly, "I've met James Thorn."

He gave a bark of laughter. "That would do it, all right." He tugged on her hair. "But you're not going to be a cop either. What you are going to be is a PI."

She felt her eyes go saucer round as her breath caught. "I'm going to be a private investigator? A *professional* private investigator?"

"*Apprentice* professional private investigator," he corrected firmly. "You've got a lot to learn, baby." His lips thinned. "Like how to think before you go off on a wild tear. Dammit, woman, when I remember the way you—"

"Wait," she said, and laid her hand over his mouth. "Wait." Dreams were coming true right and left, and she felt a little dizzy.

She closed her eyes, drew a deep breath, and opened them again. "I'm going to be a private investigator. I have a lot to learn." She shook her head, trying to take it all in. "Who's going to teach me?"

"Me." He shrugged. "Well, me and Gebhardt. We came up with the idea while we were planted in that damn cornfield last night. Our own agency. So how about it, sweetheart? You want in?"

He looked entirely too sure of himself, but she

wasn't going to be that easy. Her eyes narrowed shrewdly. "I want to be an equal partner with you and Geb," she said, and almost laughed out loud when she got the predictable scowl.

"Come on, Candy, you know better than that. You can't be an equal partner."

"Why not?"

"Experience."

"What about it?"

"You don't have any," he reminded her smugly. "Geb and I have years of it."

It was a valid argument, one that had her lips moving into a pout before she brightened. "Yes, but I've got something even better than experience."

He looked wary. "What's that?"

"I've got you," she purred, and lowered herself on top of him with a provocative wriggle that made his eyes narrow. "Right here. At my mercy."

"You're going to fight dirty, aren't you?" he growled as she ran her tongue under his jaw.

"It's one of my best qualities." Her teeth raked his collarbone, and he shuddered.

"Go ahead and argue your case, baby. . . ." He caught her lips for a quick, fierce kiss. "But I haven't changed my mind."

"But I'm not done arguing," she murmured, and flicked her tongue over his nipple.

"I hope not," he groaned.

"I really should be a partner, Hunter." She nibbled across his chest, thoroughly arousing both him and herself in the process. "It's only right," she explained as she urged him onto his side and slid her leg over his hip.

Except all of a sudden he was pushing inside her and she couldn't remember *what* was only right, because her heart was pounding and she wanted him again.

"Later," he ground out. "We can negotiate contracts later. Please."

Candy lifted her mouth for a kiss. "All right, later."

It was much, much later when she finally stirred. Stirring took quite a bit of effort. "Hunter?"

"Hmm?"

"Are you all right?"

"Hmm."

"Hunter?"

Big sigh. "What?"

"I don't think we're . . . well, normal. Three times in a row, Hunter?"

"Yeah, it's a record for me too." They thought about it for a minute, then he shrugged. "Don't fret, baby, we'll probably slow down some when we're sixty or so."

Okay, that sounded reasonable. Besides, there was another matter to settle. "Hunter?"

He groaned. "Don't you ever sleep, woman?"

"In a minute. About that partnership . . ."

"Like a damn terrier," he muttered. "I've been awake for over twenty-four hours. I'm beat and I want to go to sleep. If I agree to make you a *junior* partner, will you let me go to sleep?

"Yes," she said promptly, kissed his chin, and snuggled closer. His breathing quickly evened into the rhythm of sleep, and she smiled.

She stared out the window, watching the day age as the sun moved across the sky in slow degrees, loving Hunter and dreaming of the long, exciting future she was going to have with him.

Her body craved sleep, but logistics kept her mind humming. There was a mind-boggling list of to dos if they were going to leave by the end of the week, and she was determined to leave no later than that. But first she had to call her family, put the house up for sale, pack up the things she wanted to move to Hunter's . . . well, wherever he lived, and sell the rest.

There would be no two weeks' notice for Carmichael, she thought, gloating, but James Thorn had assured her that Karl Nelson's sojourn in Anaheim had left him tan and fit. Good. Tan, fit Karl could take on the combined girls' and boys' gym classes for a while. She was outta there.

She and Hunter would probably live and work in L.A. Sin City, she thought, and grinned. Business would be brisk, with never a dull moment. And if she ever did encounter the stray dull moment—something she couldn't imagine with Hunter around—she'd just pop over to Beverly Hills and visit her friend Jen Maddox and her hunk of a husband, Brent.

Life with Hunter, she mused, would never lack spice.

And now that she had it all planned out, she started to dream about the wedding.

Small, she decided, and the sooner they could get to Vegas, the better. Imagining Hunter looking tall and good enough to eat in a black suit had her sighing lustily.

He was actually going to be hers. For a lifetime.

She could almost picture the ceremony that would make them man and wife. The little wedding chapel in Vegas, the preacher standing in front of them wreathed in smiles and dressed in an off-the-rack, three-piece suit.

Closing her eyes, she murmured dreamily, "I, Candy Johnson, take you, Hunter—"

The blank that followed jarred her eyes open again. She shook her head with a short, disbelieving laugh. "I'm going to marry the man, and I don't even know his last name." Rolling onto her side, she gave his arm a shake. "Hunter?"

His head wagged on the pillow as he mumbled, "Later, baby. Too tired now."

"One-track mind." She sighed, and shook him harder. "Hunter! Wake up a minute."

He turned away from her. "Uh-uh."

"Just one more question."

Tugged the pillow over his head. "No."

Candy lifted the pillow just far enough to expose an ear. "Come on, Hunter, this is important. Tell me your last name, and I'll leave you alone."

"Promise?"

"Cross my heart."

"Kane. It's Kane," he muttered, and pulled the pillow back into place.

Candy's lips moved soundlessly, formed the name.

Kane? His last name was Kane? No, that couldn't be right, because that would make her . . . "Mrs. Hunter Kane, a.k.a.—"

She couldn't say it. She just couldn't.

Maybe he wouldn't mind if she kept her maiden name, she thought desperately. Lots of women did that nowadays. Then she looked at him and sighed, because she knew she could never bring herself to ask him.

He could be arrogant and bossy, but he knew her better than anyone else on earth. And because he loved her as completely as he knew her, he would suppress his protective streak—no easy task because the darned thing was about a mile wide—to give her the kind of exciting career she'd always wanted.

He was so generous in his love, and yet he'd been shocked and desperately uncertain when he found out she loved him. Hadn't anybody ever said *I love you* to him before? Just the thought had angry tears springing into her eyes. Well, somebody would damn well say it to him every day from now on, she vowed fiercely.

She loved him so much she ached with it. She wanted to share his life and have his babies. And she wanted to take his name.

Candy closed her eyes on a defeated sigh, resigned to her future as the butt of jokes, puns, and wisecracks. Hunter was worth it, she mused sleepily, draping her arm over his broad chest.

So for Hunter, and only for Hunter, she'd be Candy Kane and like it.

THE EDITORS' CORNER

The new year is once again upon us, and we're ushering it in with four new LOVESWEPTs to grace your bookshelves. From the mountains of Kentucky and Nevada to the beaches of Florida, we'll take you to places only your heart can go! So curl up in a comfy chair and hide out from the rest of the world while you plan a christening party with Peggy, catch a killer with Ruth, rescue a pirate with Cynthia, and camp out in the Sierras with Jill.

First is **ANGELS ON ZEBRAS**, LOVESWEPT #866, by the well-loved Peggy Webb. Attorney Joseph Patrick Beauregard refuses to allow Maxie Corban to include zebras at their godson's christening party. Inappropriate, he says. And that's just the beginning! Joe likes his orderly life just fine, and Maxie can't help but try to shake it up by playing the brazen hussy to Joe's conservative legal eagle. Suffice it to say, a steamy yet tenuous relationship ensues, as they learn they can't keep their hands off each other! You may remember Joe and Maxie's relatives as B. J. Corban and Crash Beauregard from BRINGING UP BAXTER, LOVESWEPT #847. Peggy Webb stuns us with another sensual tale of love and laughter in this enchanting mix of sizzle and whimsy.

Ex-cop Rafe Ramirez has no choice but to become the hero of a little girl determined to save her mom in Ruth Owen's **SOMEONE TO WATCH OVER ME**, LOVESWEPT #867. TV anchorwoman Tory Chandler has been receiving dangerous riddles and rhymes written in bloodred ink. Knowing her past is about to rear its ugly head, she wants nothing more than to ignore the threats that have her on edge. Rafe can't ignore them, however, since he's given Tory's daughter his word. Protecting the beautiful temptress who so openly betrayed him is the hardest assignment he's ever had to face. Now that he's back on the road to recovery, can this compassionate warrior keep Tory safe from her worst nightmares? LOVESWEPT favorite Ruth Owen explores the healing of two wounded souls in this story of dark emotions and desperate yearnings.

In **YOUR PLACE OR MINE?**, LOVESWEPT #868, by Cynthia Powell, Captain Diego Swift wakes to find himself stranded in a time much different from his own, and becomes engaged in an argument with the demure she-devil who has besieged his home. Catalina Steadwell had prayed for help from above, though admittedly this half-drowned, naked sailor was not what she was expecting. Though Cat doesn't believe this man's ravings about the nineteenth century, she does need a man around her dilapidated house, and hires Diego as her handyman. After all, the job market for pirates has pretty much dwindled to nothing. When Diego becomes involved in a local gang war, he learns to make use of his second chance at life and love. Here's a positively scrumptious tale by Cynthia Powell that's sure to fulfill every woman's dream of a seafaring, swashbuckling hero!

In **SHOW ME THE WAY,** LOVESWEPT #869, by Jill Shalvis, Katherine Wilson ventures into the wilds of the high Sierras in a desperate attempt to stay alive. Outfitter Kyle Spencer challenges the pretty prosecutor to accompany his group in conquering the elements, but Katy is a city girl at heart. As danger stalks them through God's country, suddenly nothing in the woods is as innocent as it seems. Kyle knows that something is terrifying Katy and wants desperately to help her, but how can he when the woman won't let him near her? Their attraction grows as their time together ebbs, and soon Katy will have to make a choice. Will she entrust Kyle with her life and her heart, or will the maniac who's after her succeed in destroying her? In this journey of survival and discovery, Jill Shalvis shows us once again how believing in love can save you from yourself.

Happy reading!

With warmest wishes,

Susann Brailey

Joy Abella

Susann Brailey　　　　　Joy Abella

Senior Editor　　　　　　Administrative Editor

P.S. Look for these Bantam women's fiction titles coming in January! National bestseller Patricia Potter delivers **STARCATCHER.** On the eve before Lady Marsali Mackey's wedding, she is kidnapped by Patrick Sutherland, Earl of Trydan, and the man who had promised to marry her twelve years ago. And Lisa Gardner, who may be familiar as Silhouette author Alicia Scott, makes her chilling suspense debut with **THE PERFECT HUSBAND,** a novel about a woman who teams up with a mercenary to catch a serial killer. And immediately following this page, preview the Bantam women's fiction titles on sale in November!

For current information on Bantam's women's fiction, visit our new Web site, *Isn't It Romantic,* at the following address:

http://www.bdd.com/romance

Don't miss these extraordinary books
from your favorite Bantam authors!

On sale in November:

TIDINGS OF GREAT JOY
by Sandra Brown

LONG AFTER MIDNIGHT
by Iris Johansen

TABOO
by Susan Johnson

STOLEN MOMENTS
by Michelle Martin

Now in paperback!

LONG AFTER MIDNIGHT

by *New York Times* bestselling author

Iris Johansen

The first warning was triggered hundreds of miles away. The second warning exploded only yards from where she and her son stood. Now Kate Denby realizes the frightening truth: She is somebody's target.

Danger has arrived in Kate's backyard with a vengeance. And the gifted scientist is awakening to a nightmare world where a ruthless killer is stalking her . . . where her innocent son is considered expendable . . . and where the medical research to which she has devoted her life is the same research that could get her killed. Her only hope of protecting her family and making that medical breakthrough is to elude her enemy until she can face him on her own ground, on her own terms—and destroy him.

Joshua remained awake for almost an hour, and even after his eyes finally closed, he slept fitfully.

It was just as well they were going away, Kate thought. Joshua wasn't a high-strung child, but what he'd gone through was enough to unsettle anyone.

Phyliss's door was closed, Kate noted when she reached the hall. She should probably get to bed too. Not that she'd be able to sleep. She hadn't lied to Joshua; she was nervous and uneasy . . . and bitterly resentful. This was her home, it was supposed to be a haven. She didn't like to think of it as a fortress.

But, like it or not, it was a fortress at the moment and she'd better make sure the soldiers were on the battlements. She checked the lock on the front door before she moved quickly toward the living room. She would see the black-and-white from the picture window.

Phyliss, as usual, had drawn the drapes over the window before she went to bed. The cave instinct, Kate thought as she reached for the cord. Close out the outside world and make your own. She and Phyliss were in complete agree—

He was standing outside the window, so close they were separated only by a quarter of an inch of glass.

Oh God. High concave cheekbones, long black straight hair drawn back in a queue, beaded necklace. It was him . . . Ishmaru.

And he was smiling at her.

His lips moved and he was so near she could hear the words through the glass. "You weren't supposed to see me before I got in, Kate." He held her gaze as he showed her the glass cutter in his hand. "But it's all right. I'm almost finished and I like it better this way."

She couldn't move. She stared at him, mesmerized.

"You might as well let me in. You can't stop me."

She jerked the drapes shut, closing him out.

Barricading herself inside with only a fragment of glass, a scrap of material . . .

She heard the sound of blade on glass.

She backed away from the window, stumbled on the hassock, almost fell, righted herself.

Oh God. Where was that policeman? The porch light was out, but surely he could see Ishmaru.

Maybe the policeman wasn't there.

And your husband never mentioned bribery in the ranks?

The drapes were moving.

He'd cut the window.

"Phyliss!" She ran down the hall. "Wake up." She threw open Joshua's door, flew across the room, and jerked him out of bed.

"Mom?"

"Shh, be very quiet. Just do what I tell you, okay?"

"What's wrong?" Phyliss was standing in the doorway. "Is Joshua sick?"

"I want you to leave here." She pushed Joshua toward her. "There's someone outside." She hoped he was still outside. Christ, he could be in the living room by now. "I want you to take Joshua out the back door and over to the Brocklemans'."

Phyliss instantly took Joshua's hand and moved toward the kitchen door. "What about you?"

She heard a sound in the living room. "*Go.* I'll be right behind you."

Phyliss and Joshua flew out the back door.

"Are you waiting for me, Kate?"

He sounded so close, too close. Phyliss and Joshua could not have reached the fence yet. No time to run. Stop him.

She saw him, a shadow in the doorway leading to the hall.

Where was the gun?

In her handbag on the living room table. She couldn't get past him. She backed toward the stove.

Phyliss usually left a frying pan out to cook breakfast in the morning. . . .

"I told you I was coming in. No one can stop me tonight. I had a sign."

She didn't see a weapon but the darkness was lit only by moonlight streaming through the window.

"Give up, Kate."

Her hand closed on the handle of the frying pan. "Leave me *alone*." She leaped forward and struck out at his head with all her strength.

He moved too fast but she connected with a glancing blow.

He was falling. . . .

She streaked past him down the hall. Get to the purse, the gun.

She heard him behind her.

She snatched up the handbag, lunged for the door, and threw the bolt.

Get to the policeman in the black-and-white.

She fumbled with the catch on her purse as she streaked down the driveway toward the black-and-white. Her hand closed on the gun and she threw the purse aside.

"He's not there, Kate," Ishmaru said behind her. "It's just the two of us."

"Susan Johnson's love scenes sparkle, sizzle,
and burn!" —*Affaire de Coeur*

Through eleven nationally bestselling books, award
winner Susan Johnson has won a legion of fans for
her lushly romantic historical novels. Now she
delivers her most thrilling tale yet—a searing blend
of rousing adventure and wild, forbidden love . . .

TABOO

by Susan Johnson

*Married against her will to the brutal Russian general
who conquered her people, Countess Teo Korsakova has
never known what it means to want a man . . . until
now. Trapped behind enemy lines, held captive by her husband's most formidable foe, she should fear for her life. But
all Teo feels in General Andre Duras's shattering presence
is breathless passion. France's most victorious commander,
Andre knows that he should do the honorable thing, knows
too that on the eve of battle he cannot afford so luscious a
distraction. Yet something about Teo lures him to do the
unthinkable: to seduce his enemy's wife, and to let himself
love a woman who can never be his.*

He played chess the way he approached warfare, moving quickly, decisively, always on the attack. But she
held her own, although her style was less aggressive,
and when he took her first knight after long conten-
tion for its position, he said, "If your husband's half as
good as you, he'll be a formidable opponent."

"I'm not sure you fight the same way."

"You've seen him in battle?"

"On a small scale. Against my grandfather in Siberia."

"And yet you married him?"

"Not by choice. The Russians traditionally take hostages from their conquered tribes. I'm the Siberian version. My clan sends my husband tribute in gold each year. So you see why I'm valuable to him."

"Not for gold alone, I'm sure," he said, beginning to move his rook.

"How gallant, Andre," she playfully declared.

His gaze came up at the sound of his name, his rook poised over the board, and their glances held for a moment. The fire crackled noisily in the hearth, the ticking of the clock sounded loud in the stillness, the air suddenly took on a charged hush, and then the general smiled—a smooth, charming smile. "You're going to lose your bishop, Teo."

She couldn't answer as suavely because her breath was caught in her throat and it took her a second to overcome the strange, heated feeling inundating her senses.

His gaze slid down her blushing cheeks and throat to rest briefly on her taut nipples visible through her white cashmere robe and he wondered what was happening to him that so demure a sight had such a staggering effect on his libido. He dropped his rook precipitously into place, inhaled, and leaned back in his chair, as if putting distance between himself and such tremulous innocence would suffice to restore his reason.

"Your move," he gruffly said.

"Maybe we shouldn't play anymore."

"Your move." It was his soft voice of command.

"I don't take orders."

"I'd appreciate it if you'd move."

"I'm not sure I know what I'm doing anymore." He lounged across from her, tall, lean, powerful, with predatory eyes, the softest of voices, and the capacity to make her tremble.

"It's only a game."

"This, you mean."

"Of course. What else would I mean?"

"I was married when I was fifteen, after two years of refinement at the Smolny Institute for Noble Girls," she pertinently said, wanting him to know.

"And you're very refined," he urbanely replied, wondering how much she knew of love after thirteen faithful years in a forced marriage. His eyes drifted downward again, his thoughts no longer of chess.

"My husband's not refined at all."

"Many Russians aren't." He could feel his erection begin to rise, the thought of showing her another side of passionate desire ruinous to his self-restraint.

"It's getting late," she murmured, her voice quavering slightly.

"I'll see you upstairs," he softly said.

When he stood, his desire was obvious; the form-fitting regimentals molded his body like a second skin.

Gripping the chair arms, she said, "No," her voice no more than a whisper.

He moved around the small table and touched her then because he couldn't help himself, because she was quivering with desire like some virginal young girl and the intoxicating image of such tremulous need was more carnal than anything he'd ever experienced. His hand fell lightly on her shoulder, its heat tantalizing, tempting.

She looked up at him and, lifting her mouth to his, heard herself say, "Kiss me."

"Take my hand," he murmured. And when she did, he pulled her to her feet and drew her close so the scent of her was in his nostrils and the warmth of her body touched his.

"Give me a child." Some inner voice prompted the words she'd only dreamed for years.

"No," he calmly said, as if she hadn't asked the unthinkable from a stranger, and then his mouth covered hers and she sighed against his lips. And as their kiss deepened and heated their blood and drove away reason, they both felt an indefinable bliss—torrid and languorous, heartfelt and, most strangely—hopeful in two people who had long ago become disenchanted with hope.

And then her maid's voice drifted down the stairway, the intonation of her native tongue without inflection. "He'll kill you," she declared.

Duras's mouth lifted and his head turned to the sound. "What did she say?"

"She reminded me of the consequences."

"Which are?"

"My husband's wrath."

He was a hairsbreadth from selfishly saying, *Don't worry*, but her body had gone rigid in his arms at her maid's pointed admonition and at base he knew better. He knew he wouldn't be there to protect her from her husband's anger and he knew too that she was much too innocent for a casual night of love.

"Tamyr is my voice of reason."

He released her and took a step away, as if he couldn't trust himself to so benignly relinquish such powerful feeling. "We all need a voice of reason," he neutrally said. "Thank you for the game of chess."

"I'm sorry."

"Not more sorry than I," Duras said with a brief smile.

"Will I see you again?" She couldn't help herself from asking.

"Certainly." He took another step back, his need for her almost overwhelming. "And if you wish for anything during your stay with us, feel free to call on Bonnay."

"Can't I call on you?"

"My schedule's frenzied and, more precisely, your maid's voice may not be able to curtail me a second time."

"I see."

"Forgive my bluntness."

"Forgiven," she gently said.

"Good night, Madame Countess." He bowed with grace.

"Good night, Andre."

"Under other circumstances . . ." he began, and then shrugged away useless explanation.

"I know," she softly said. "Thank you."

He left precipitously, retreat uncommon for France's bravest general, but he wasn't sure he could trust himself to act the gentleman if he stayed.

"Michelle Martin writes fresh, funny, fast-paced contemporary romance with a delicious hint of suspense."
—Teresa Medeiros, nationally bestselling author of *Touch of Enchantment*

The irresistible Michelle Martin, author of *Stolen Hearts*, whips up a delectable new concoction of a woman chasing a dream . . . and the man who fulfills her sweetest fantasies . . .

STOLEN MOMENTS

by Michelle Martin

It was just after midnight when the Princess of Pop made her escape, leaving behind the syrupy-sweet ballads and the tyrannical manager who had made her famous. All Harley Jane Miller wanted was a vacation: two weeks on her own in New York before recording her next album. Yet now that she's tasted freedom, the Princess of Pop's gone electric: changing her clothes, her music, and her good-girl image. And she's never going back. Harley knows it will take some quick thinking to shake her greedy manager. But she never suspects she'll be waylaid by a diamond heist, the French mafia, and a devastatingly gorgeous detective who's determined to bring her in—by way of his bedroom . . . and when he does, Harley Jane will be more than willing to comply . . .

"Hello again, Miss Miller."

Harley's heart stopped. There was a roaring in her

ears. Slowly she turned her head and looked up. A man stood beside her bench. It was the hunk from Manny's, and he knew who she was. Staring up into those dark eyes, she knew it was futile for her to even attempt to pretend that she didn't know that he knew who she was. "Are you Duncan Lang, the man who was asking questions about me at the RIHGA yesterday?"

"One and the same."

"Did Boyd send you?"

"Boyd *hired* me. I found you thanks to high technology and brilliant deductive reasoning."

Harley stared up at him. "Can you be bought off?"

His dark eyes crinkled in amusement. " 'Fraid not. Dad would be peeved. Colangco has a sterling reputation for honesty and results. Sorry," he said as he picked up her Maxi-Mouse. "Shall we head back to the Hilton for your things?"

Crud, he knew where she was staying. Harley tried to think, but her brain felt like iced sludge. It was over. She hadn't even had two full days of freedom yet, and it was over.

Her chest ached. "I'm twenty-six, a grown woman, legally independent," she stated. "You can't just haul me back to Boyd like he *owns* me!"

"I can when that's what I'm hired to do."

"But I haven't even had a chance to try out my new guitar," Harley said, hot tears welling in her eyes. She hurriedly pushed them back. "Boyd is not about to let me keep it. He hates electric guitars. He doesn't think they're feminine."

"What?"

"And he won't let me wear black clothes, or red

clothes, or anything resembling a bright color. And no jeans. Not even slacks."

"He's got a tight rein on you," Duncan Lang agreed as he sat down beside her.

"He is sucking the life's blood out of me."

"Why do you let him?"

"Boyd is deaf to anyone's 'no' except his own," Harley replied bitterly.

"But as you pointed out, you are twenty-six and legally independent. You don't have to put up with his crap if you don't want to."

"Why do you care?" Harley demanded, glaring up at the treacherous hunk.

"I don't," Duncan Lang stated. "I'm just curious. You did a very good job of hiding yourself among eight million people—"

"*You* found me."

"Ah, well," he said, ducking his head in false modesty, "I'm a trained investigator, after all." His winsome smile must have charmed every female who'd even glanced at him sideways from the time he was sixteen. It made Harley's teeth grate. "My point is that," he continued, "Boyd's opinion notwithstanding, you seem fully capable of taking care of yourself. Fire the control freak and get on with your life."

"It's not that easy," Harley said, her arms tightening around the guitar case. "I owe everything to Boyd: my career, my success, my fame, my money. I'd still be a little hick from Oklahoma if it weren't for him. And I'm not so sure I can make it in the industry without him now."

"He *has* run a number on you, hasn't he?"

"Oh yeah," Harley said, staring down at the concrete ground.

"So why did you run away?"

Harley felt her stomach freeze over. Her jaws began to liquefy. She stared blindly at the fountain. "The music stopped coming," she whispered.

"I thought so," Duncan Lang said.

Harley turned her head and met his sympathetic black gaze. It nearly undid her. Oh God, her music! "It's been two months and not a note, not a lyric." The well she had depended on all of her life had gone dry. There was nothing left to be tapped. She looked up at him, pleading for a stay of execution. "I thought if I could just have a few weeks of fun. A few weeks of not being Jane Miller. A few weeks of just letting go, and maybe it would come back. Maybe I'd be okay again. Then I'd fly to L.A., get back on the treadmill, and make the damn album for Sony."

Harley almost clapped a hand to her mouth. Years ago Boyd had forbidden Jane Miller to swear in public or private.

"A reasonable plan," Lang agreed.

"Then let me go!" Harley said, her hand clutching his arm. "Let me have my two weeks. No one will be hurt. I'll come back and fulfill all of my obligations, I promise."

"Sorry, Princess, that's not part of the plan."

"Who the *hell* do you think you are?" Harley exploded. "You're not God. You have no right to tell me where to go or what to do. I'll fly off to *Brazil* if I feel like it and you can't stop me."

"Oh yes I can," he retorted.

"How?"

"By physical force if necessary."

He looked like he could do it too. "*Oh*, I hate men," Harley seethed. "The arrogance. The stupidity."

"I'm actually pretty intelligent," Duncan Lang retorted, dark eyes glittering. "Don't forget, I found you."

"If you found me, you can lose me."

"No."

"Dammit, Lang—"

"I signed a contract, Princess. I am obligated to fulfill it."

"But not today," Harley pleaded. "You don't have to fulfill it today, or tomorrow, or even a week from tomorrow. Give me back my holiday, Mr. Lang."

He looked down at her. A gamine with breasts, dressed all in black. He'd known an odd kind of fascination as he'd surreptitiously watched her in Manny's Music. She had a quality . . . like Sleeping Beauty just waking up from a hundred years' sleep and discovering the world anew.

He'd never felt that kind of immediate attraction to a woman in his life. Oh sure, he'd been drawn to beautiful women, and voluptuous women, and even bewitching women. Harley was none of those things. She was just somehow . . . familiar.

"Okay, Princess, here's the deal," he said with sudden decision. "I'll do a little digging while you make like a tourist or a musician or whatever the hell it is you want to be today. But at midnight I put you back in your pumpkin and return you to Mr. Monroe." Duncan held out his hand. "Deal?"

Faux brown eyes stared up at him a moment. Then Harley Jane Miller's slim fingers slid across his hand, clasping it firmly, disconcerting him with a sudden feeling of connection. "Deal."

DON'T MISS THESE FABULOUS
BANTAM WOMEN'S FICTION TITLES

DON'T MISS ANY OF THESE EXTRAORDINARY BANTAM NOVELS

On Sale in December

THE PERFECT HUSBAND
by LISA GARDNER

A terrifying paperback debut about a woman who
put her husband behind bars, became his next target
when he broke out, and had to learn to fight back
to save her own life—this un-put-down-able
novel is a non-stop thrill ride!

____ 57680-1 $6.50/$8.99 in Canada

STARCATCHER
by PATRICIA POTTER

A powerful story in which war and
feuding families conspire to keep apart two lovers
who have been betrothed for twelve years.
But, like Romeo and Juliet, they are determined
to honor a love meant to be.

____ 57507-4 $5.99/$7.99 in Canada